2 SIDES OF A PENNY
Part 2

Carlton Brown

Life Changing Books
Published by Life Changing Books
P.O. Box 423
Brandywine, MD 20613

This novel is a work of fiction. Any references to real people, events, establishments, or locales are intended only to give the fiction a sense of reality and authenticity. Other names, characters, and incidents occurring in the work are either the product of the author's imagination or are used fictitiously, as are those fictionalized events and incidents that involve real persons. Any character that happens to share the name of a person who is an acquaintance of the author, past or present, is purely coincidental and is in no way intended to be an actual account involving that person.

Library of Congress Cataloging-in-Publication Data;

www.lifechangingbooks.net

13 Digit: 9781943174058

Follow Us:

Twitter: www.twitter.com/lcbooks
Facebook: Life Changing Books/lcbooks
Instagram: Lcbooks
Pinterest: Life Changing Books

DEDICATION

Wow, this has been an amazing ride. Thank you to all the people who supported me and LC Books with their purchase of part one. I am truly humbled by all the kind words and great feedback I have received from all of you. I really, really appreciate it all. There is something to be said about being respected for your words and creative vision.

My plan from the gate was to put the readers in a place of page turning when opening one of my books. I wanted it to be all the way realistic with no fakery or made up fluff. I wanted you all to feel like you're watching a movie. To connect with every character and either love them or hate them or cry for them. I have received all of the above in the feeds from part 1 so part 2 is dedicated to the readers and those who support this quest.

I'm truly thankful for you all and I hope you love every book I put out and I keep you entertained. Peace to the struggle for without it, we would learn nothing. Be blessed.

Follow me: @CarlBDreamKings

Much respect,

Carlton Brown

CHAPTER 1

Savion flew through red lights at each corner without a care in the world. A bottle of Moët Rosé rested between his thighs as his speed increased down Foothill Boulevard.

"What you mean the nigga don't have the money?" he screamed into his phone.

Keisha paid him no attention as she flipped through a CD case, casually looking out into Oakland's hidden darkness as the city lights gleamed off Savion's chrome 24-inch rims.

Keisha felt on top of the world, thinking about the life she had down in Fresno, compared to the life she had temporarily experienced in Oakland. Glancing over at Savion, Keisha thought about all the cute guys that would be at the party their neighbor had told her about. Just like any other city in the country, men could smell new pussy like a bloodhound to a dead body. In Oakland, the mind frame of young men was always pimp or die, so no one cared if Keisha had a man. All they cared about was the vulnerability she gave off every time somebody spoke to her.

While Savion would run the streets all day, Keisha would be busy flirting with any and every man she thought to be cute. Being a California country girl, all the game flying off their slick tongues seemed like the gospel to a soul in need of saving. Keisha was hypnotized by all of the jewelry and endless mounds of confidence, plus excitement each of them held. The same things that attracted her to Savion, was all over and right in her face twenty-four seven.

Keisha twisted her thick lips as she leaned over and began kissing Savion on his neck. Savion continued punching the gas pedal in his Navigator while still talking on the phone.

"Let me call you back, my nigga. I'm 'bout to get some head from my bitch. I'll hit you after the party. Make sure that nigga gives you that money. Don't take no for an answer."

Savion tossed the phone over his shoulder as he slowed to let his seat back a bit while Keisha ran her long slippery tongue all over his neck while massaging his dick through his pants.

"Girl, what you trying to get started?" Savion said, unbuckling his Ed Hardy jeans.

Keisha put her hand in his pants and began slowly, sensually, massaging his dick. Savion leaned back further and slowed at a red light on 73rd street. East Oakland was alive and brewing. Savion let his window down as the light turned green.

"What it do?" he yelled to the youngsters on the corner of 76th street.

Everyone looked, but no one spoke as Savion continued pushing down the street. Keisha put her big high yellow booty up in the air for everyone to see as she began licking and sucking Savion's dick.

"Yeeeeee!" Savion screamed out the window as Keisha worked her magic.

Savion pulled over on 78th street in front of Jimmies Market where the 700 bang gang held down the front and the rest of the block.

Keisha sucked with passion, as she knew she was drawing an audience. Youngsters and old heads alike crowded around the Navigator, watching Keisha as Savion threw up his hands, loving all of the attention.

Camera phones of all kinds were out, capturing the moment. Savion leaned into one of them, grinning ear to ear.

"This is what it's all about, niggas. Get your money up, and then get ya' pussy up niggas. Look at the work this bitch do. Say hi, baby."

Keisha sucked hard once as she looked up into the camera.

"Hi," she said, while waving and going back down on his dick.

Savion laughed as he put the car in drive and crept off. Keisha looked up as Savion parked in front of the house the party was at on Idlewood, right off of 82nd street. Keisha continued sucking while Savion popped an ecstasy pill, watching everyone lounging outside and those headed into the house.

"That's enough," he said, pushing Keisha's head away from him. Keisha sucked hard one more time as she sat up in the truck.

Keisha held her tongue out and Savion put an ecstasy pill in her mouth.

"Thank you, daddy! I can't wait till this kick in."

"Well, you better stay close to me. I don't want yo' young hot ass in there acting like you just get down with anybody. You better let these niggas know who daddy is, and if you want to get down with anybody, you already know to have a fee. So get the money or stay close to me."

Keisha rolled her eyes as Savion buttoned his pants and stepped out of the truck. Keisha straightened out her skirt and joined him.

Savion shook hands with everyone as they entered the house. Everyone knew he was crazy, but the respect made Savion feel like the world was his. Keisha sucked in all of the attention as every man in the room was stuck on her long weave and high yellow curves. Savion felt the pill kick in as his mood became a little more intense.

Keisha caught the eye of a tall skinny guy across the room. Standing next to Savion, she continued to make eyes with the guy as Savion bragged about the head game he was getting on the way over. Standing six feet tall with a mocha brown complexion, Keisha was drawn into his smooth smile and wide, deep sunken eyes.

Ballers from all over the town stood around, with beautiful women in front of them or hanging from their arms.

Savion stood at a table, snorting a line of coke, while Keisha tried to search through the crowd for the tall, wide-eyed brother. Savion swung her around and stuck his tongue down her throat. "Damn, I wanna fuck the shit out of you," he whispered in her ear over the pounding speakers.

Keisha licked her lips as Savion snorted another line. Keisha knew the coke made him horny, so she looked around for a corner or a room to do the business.

"Sav, what's good my nigga?" a loud booming voice yelled from behind them.

Keisha turned around to see the tall brother standing in all his finesse, right before her. Savion wiped his nose and hugged him.

"What it do, Neiff? It's been a minute, my nigga. What you been into?"

Neiff was a baller from the notorious 69 Vill. He and Savion often crossed paths whenever Savion wasn't in prison. Neiff pulled at the collar of his white on green Gino Green Global track jacket as Keisha looked him up and down.

"Ah, you know, nigga, a little of this and that. Shit still the same. Who's the bitch you got with you?" Neiff whispered into Savion's ear.

Savion smiled as he leaned down to take another toot, watching Keisha eye fuck Neiff.

"You like that, huh?"

Neiff nodded his head.

Savion wiped his nose off before slapping Keisha on the butt. "This my bitch, blood. She can't be touched unless the price is right, so what you talking?"

"I ain't talking shit if you trying to get me to be a trick, nigga. I mack bitches, I don't pay them for shit. Nigga they pay me."

"Well that's the only way you touching this one, cuzzin'."

Neiff cracked his wide smooth smile at Keisha before parting ways.

"Niggas always want some shit for free," Savion said, popping another pill.

Neiff stood a few feet away, still watching Keisha. Keisha played with her tongue as Savion began slamming shots of Patron.

"I'm ready to fuck, bitch. You ready?"

Keisha rolled her eyes as she nodded her head, while Neiff shot her a 'come here' glance and nodded his head towards the bathroom.

"I gotta go to the bathroom, baby. I'll be right back."

"Hurry up, bitch. I'm ready to get up out of here."

"Already? We just got here."

"Bitch, don't ask no questions. I handled my business already, and I'm ready to get you to the house and fuck the shit of you. You know that's what your freak ass wants."

Keisha stood by, feeling less of a woman as Savion degraded her.

"Ok, Sav, if that's what you want."

"Yeah, it's what I want, bitch. Now hurry up."

Keisha watched as Neiff got everyone out of the bathroom. Quickly, she made her way there as Savion began talking to another guy who had approached them. After maneuvering her way through the crowd of people, Keisha finally made her way to the bathroom. Neiff waited inside, leaning against the sink as Keisha came in and shut the door behind her.

"What's up, baby?" Neiff said, grabbing her by the waist.

Keisha felt powerless in his arms as she let nature take its course.

"Nothing, I just had been checking you out the whole night. You got a real smooth swag that I'm feeling to the fullest, daddy."

"Is that right? You know you need to be over here dealing

with a real nigga rather than wasting your time with that chump ass nigga, Sav. He ain't gone do nothing but go back to jail as soon as the coke and his attitude catch up with him."

Keisha pursed her lips at the thought of Savion going to jail.

"Well, if and when that happens, I know where to find you. What's your name?"

"Neiff. Everybody calls me that. I don't tell anybody my real name."

Keisha tossed back the hair from her face.

"Damn, you fine as fuck, girl. I want to do some things to you right now."

"Well, what you waiting on? Savion is waiting on me so we can leave, so you have to make it fast."

Neiff unbuckled his pants and pulled out his 10-inch dick as Keisha knelt down on the floor.

"Damn daddy, you working with a little too much. Let me see what I can do with this," she said as she began to suck slowly with a whole lot of spit.

Neiff braced himself on the sink as Keisha's jaws became stronger with every stroke. Neiff let his head fall to his neck as the feeling became too good.

Keisha looked up at him, wanting to feel him deep inside of her. Neiff stood her up and bent her over the sink as he took time to put his condom on.

"Hurry up, daddy," Keisha said.

"Shut up, bitch. Be still while I give you this dick."

Just as she was about to say something, Neiff shoved his dick deep inside her wet inviting pussy. Keisha gasped and gripped tight to the sink as Neiff pushed his dick as far as it would go.

Meanwhile, Savion slammed another shot with the same person he was talking to when Keisha left ten minutes prior. Checking his watch while looking around, Savion noticed the bathroom door still closed.

"Man, this bitch taking forever," he cut into his boy's

conversation. "I'll holler at you later."

Savion slammed one more shot before making his way through the crowd. The room became blurry as the pills and alcohol began to blend together. Savion braced himself at the door, trying to gather his vision and balance. Shaking it away, he turned the knob and stepped in.

"Damn bitch, what's taking so damn…"

Keisha and Neiff jumped at the sound of his voice.

Savion stood in pure shock as he watched Neiff pull his dick out of Keisha's pussy as she stood bent over the sink. Savion snapped out of the shock as he pushed Neiff into the tub.

"Nigga, I told yo' punk ass what the business was. This how you want to get down?"

Neiff laughed as he got his balance and buckled his jeans. Keisha stood up, trying to pull down her skirt.

"Daddy wait, I was wrong! I -"

Savion cut her off with a swift backhand to the mouth. Keisha flew into the medicine cabinet.

Neiff laughed as he watched Savion continuously slap her.

"Don't be too hard on her, my nigga. She couldn't help it. Damn, the pussy is cream though. You got a nice one, cuzzin."

Neiff brushed past Savion as he looked at the crowd forming at the door. Savion, still fazed by the drugs, slapped Keisha again, before turning around to call Neiff.

"Aye nigga," he yelled after him.

Neiff was still laughing as he poured a shot of Patron. "What?" Neiff said before slamming the shot down.

Savion pulled out a glock from under his Ed Hardy hoody as he approached. Within a New York minute, Savion opened fire before Neiff could even sit the bottle down. Everyone in the room ducked down to the floor as the shots echoed over the bass pumping from the speakers. The shots tore through his chest and stomach five times before he dropped, with his eyes open.

"Nigga, don't you ever disrespect me," he yelled at the dead body. "That's why ya' eyes still open, nigga. You deserved that shit."

People in the party began rushing to the door as Savion marched back to the bathroom. Keisha sat on the sink holding her face as Savion stood at the door, gun at his side.

"Baby, I'm sorry," Keisha said, standing up. "I didn't mean for any of that to happen. He followed me in here right when I was about to -"

Savion licked off three shots before she could finish. Three shots echoed through the silence, ripping open Keisha's chest. A look of shock came over her face as the shots held her in one spot, not allowing her to fall. Savion held the pistol up once more and let off two more shots, knocking her back into the toilet. He turned around to look for anyone in the room, but everyone had fled from the scene, leaving him alone in the empty house. He tucked the gun in his waist and grabbed the Patron bottle as he made his way outside to his Navigator.

Italy stood in front of a floor to ceiling mirror, checking her makeup. She glanced around the room at the expensive furnishings and lavish paintings.

"Bianca? This spot is phat. What does this dude do?"

Bianca joined her in the mirror, applying her lipstick.

"Girl, unless you are about to start telling on every little thing you see, you better forget about this one and get your mind right. This fool is a district attorney."

Italy stopped in mid-stroke of her hair.

"A *District Attorney?* Girl you're playing. Oh hell naw! I'm out of here. I'm not dancing for any pigs!"

Bianca giggled to herself.

"So, are you trying to get political on me? Girl, you shake your ass for a living. You'd rather shake it for some broke niggas tipping dollars, or these white dudes breaking you off twenties or better?"

Italy stopped. She looked at Bianca as she took off her

sweatpants. Bianca stood in front of the mirror, observing herself. She pushed her breasts up and sprinkled a little glitter on her cleavage.

"Italy, break a pill in half for me. I like to feel good when a lot of money is getting passed around. Are you gone take one with me?"

Italy nodded as she split the X-pill in half. They both swallowed the halves with a chase of Hypnotic.

"Wheeeeewwww," Bianca said, slapping Italy on the butt.

"Girl, that red looks good on your yellow ass. We gone get paid tonight."

Italy giggled as she grabbed Bianca's breast.

"These things here are gonna get it all. Let's do it girl."

They opened the door and sauntered down the hall with their sexiest walks.

"Okay boys, get ready to get your minds blown," Bianca said as she stepped in the circle of men.

Italy put on their dancing music as Bianca brushed her body against each of the men. The five white men took their seats as the Ying Yang Twin's "Salt Shaker" came over the speakers. Italy and Bianca flirted with the men as they shook their bodies in harmony with the music. Italy felt the X-pill take control of her as she pulled Bianca close and kissed the tops of her breasts. The men hollered and threw more money at their feet as Bianca looked at Italy confused, but kept the flow. Lust exploded off Italy's body as they pressed their breasts together and kissed deeply.

Italy pushed back from her and stood away, spinning her hips seductively.

"Which one of you is our fine district attorney?" she asked while pressing her breasts against the face of one of the men.

The smallest man of them all stood up with a fist full of money.

"I'm right here, sugar. What you gone do for me?"

Italy pushed him onto the couch. She got on top of him as he stuffed twenty-dollar bills into her G-string while she unbuttoned his shirt and kissed his fat stomach and chest. The man didn't know what to do as Italy untied her top and let her breasts pop into his face. She let her hands roam all over his body until she was unbuckling his pants and stroking his manhood through his shorts as the rest of the men looked in awe.

"Do you like me?" Italy whispered in his ear.

"Yes, yes, yes," he moaned, stuffing all the money in his hands into her G-string.

Italy smiled and let him go to continue dancing in the middle of the room.

Bianca grabbed her from behind and massaged her breasts while licking her ear. Italy moaned loud and hard as Bianca stuck her hand between her legs and started rubbing her clitoris back and forth, slowly. The men's chants became louder, and more money was thrown at their feet.

"Damn I'm so wet," Italy whispered under her breath.

The men cleared out of the room as Italy and Bianca dressed. Bianca showered while Italy counted their money. Still feeling the pill a little, she couldn't wait to get home. A knock at the door stopped her concentration. The district attorney stood at the door smiling when she opened it.

Italy gave him a quizzical look as she spoke.

"Yes," she said, leaning against the doorframe.

"You dance real good, sugar," he said.

Italy smiled.

"Thank you."

The D.A. rubbed his baldhead as he blushed.

"Listen, I'm not going to beat around the bush. I want you, girl. I want to taste that pussy and finish what you started back there. How much? How much is it going to cost me?"

Italy couldn't believe what she was hearing. She folded

her arms over her chest as she stepped away from him.

"I don't know what you think I am, but I don't get down like that. Neither I, nor my friend does. You can keep your money, and don't ever speak to me that way again."

The chubby man turned beat red as he felt embarrassment rise to the surface of his face. Italy began to stuff clothes into their travel bag as she cursed to herself, still feeling his eyes caressing her body.

He began to laugh as she looked him in the eye.

"Sugar, it's okay now, but you'll need me before I need you. And you will give me what I want. All of you always do."

Italy felt like screaming as she heard his laughter continue down the hall. She opened the door to the bathroom as Bianca was drying off. "Girl, hurry up! Let's get the hell out of this pig's house. You won't believe what this asshole just did."

"What?" Bianca said, stepping into the room.

"I'll tell you in the car," Italy said as she threw her jeans at her.

CHAPTER 2

Bianca cracked up laughing as Italy told her what happened.

"What the hell is funny? I didn't appreciate that shit. I'm not a hoe."

Bianca grabbed her stomach as she struggled to get words out between laughter.

"You're not? What the hell do you call that shit we just did? Girl please, this is what we do. We sell sex for money. Whether it's a man sticking his dick in you or you telling him to suck your titties, we sell sex. He pays you some kind of money for a sexual act. *I ain't a hoe!* Girl please! You better just accept it. We gotta do what we have to do sometimes to get by.

"We want that Prada and Christian Dior shit. We want to drive drop mustangs and look good. You know a taste of that good life, shine better than the next bitch, so we have to do what the fuck we have to do. I wish that piggy muthafucka would've came at me with that shit. I would've charged him a thousand and sucked the skin off his dick. Shit, you fuck for free, so why not get paid for it?"

Italy gripped her steering wheel tight while Bianca laughed, watching the veins pop in Italy's forehead. She knew she was upset, but didn't care. She really liked to see Italy mad.

"Italy, please! Don't be acting all siddity all of a sudden. A few months ago, you were on the corner with all of your clothes in garbage bags. I bet you would've let a million niggas fuck you just for a place to sleep. Now you got that, and some doe in your pocket, and fucking for money is beneath you? Please! Don't get all sensitive on me now. You better keep it gangsta."

Italy stopped at a red light as Bianca turned up the Keak Da Sneak song playing in the deck. Italy turned the music back down.

"Okay, that last stuff you said might be true, but I had nothing. Yeah, I think differently now because I have a little something. I'm thinking about how to get further without lowering myself back down to that level. Bianca, think about where we could go if we put our minds on something better. A million bitches are doing this stripper shit. We could take this money and flip it into something that pays more, without losing our self-respect. This isn't going to last forever."

Bianca laughed again.

"Self-respect? You just let me stick my finger in your pussy in front of a district attorney. Miss me with that. I'm going to stretch this as far as it will go, and when it's all over, El will take care of whatever I need. He loves me and he's a genius. We're gonna stay breaded. What else are you going to do? Your dumb ass don't even have a diploma or GED-all you have is your looks. As much weed as you smoke, you probably can't even remember what happened five minutes ago."

Italy pressed on the gas pedal hard, making the car lurch forward, screeching as it went.

Bianca yelled and laughed as Italy hit the brakes at the next light.

"Oh, you mad?" she said, adjusting her seatbelt.

Italy shot the flames of hell out of her eyes.

"So what're you saying, Bianca? I'm stupid? Bitch, you don't know half the shit I've been through. I'm tired of this. I almost lost my life to a nothing ass nigga. My momma is a dope fiend. *And you*...you know what? I'm not even going to go there with you."

Bianca's smile faded.

"You can't go there. I know your ass. The rest of the girls don't know you, but I remember you letting niggas run a train on you in the bathroom at school. I remember Kamal clowning you in front of everyone. Shit, this is the best way you can stunt on everybody. This is the only way, because you can't do shit else."

Italy clenched her jaw at the memory. She remembered the feeling of just wanting to be loved and to have some attention. So she let Kamal and his friends do what they wanted with her, thinking she had proven herself worthy to be with him, only to be laughed at the next day.

As she pulled into the driveway, she tried to dismiss the thought as Bianca bounced in her seat to the music, obviously not affected by her own words.

Bianca jumped out of the car and ran into El's arms as he was walking out of the house.

"Hey baby," she said, glancing in Italy's direction while trying to kiss him. El turned his head as she aimed for his lips.

"Why are you always trying to do that shit? I told you about that. Drop it, okay?"

Bianca stood back with her hands on her hips, wanting to start fussing, but bit her tongue as El put his hand out while he dialed a number on his cell phone. Bianca stared at him as he diverted his attention towards Italy sitting on the hood of the car with a frown on her face.

"What's wrong with Italy?"

Bianca looked in her direction. "Why are you worrying about that bitch? She'll be all right. Let me worry about that."

"Hold on, Joe," said El, turning to Bianca.

"Look, I told you about questioning me. Just shut the fuck up and listen sometimes. Stop thinking you're the boss, *bitch*, and your shit don't stink. You can be replaced. And bitch, you still haven't put my damn money in my hand."

Bianca poked her lips out and reached in her bra for the money. She glanced at Italy again before putting it in his hand. El gave her a frown before walking towards Italy.

"Joe? Let me call you back."

He hung up the phone and stared at her for a second.

"What's up with you? Why are you over here mugging?"

Italy shook her head.

"Nothing baby, I'm just tired."

El nodded his head.

"Y'all got any more dates tonight?"

Italy shook her head again.

"No, that was it. Why?"

El exhaled.

"I want you to take a ride for me. I got a job for you."

"What kind of job, El?"

"What do you think? Here's the address. I'll see you later on tonight. He's going to give you $1,500.00. Bring me back $1000.00 and make him feel special."

Italy took the piece of paper, really not feeling like dancing anymore, but she didn't feel like sitting around Bianca either.

"Okay, I'll do it. I'll see you later."

El nodded at her before getting into his truck.

CHAPTER 3

The night stood still as Italy pulled up in front of a dark house. Tall palm trees lined the street of the suburban neighborhood resting in the wealthy Oakland hills. She checked the address to make sure the house was correct, as a funny feeling crept in her stomach, making her stop as she approached the door. Before she could turn around, the door opened.

"Hey, you forget something?" the deep voice said.

"No," she responded. "I was just about to check the address again. How are you doing? I'm Gemini."

"I know," he said, turning on the light to the living room. "I requested you."

Italy gladly admired his frame. *Damn, he's fine*, she thought.

"I'm Kenyan," he said, extending his hand.

"Come on in."

Italy followed him into the house.

"Your home is nice," she said, looking at the leather couches and African sculptures that accented the room around a 62-inch TV.

"Have a seat," Kenyan said, lowering the lights.

Italy put her bags down and took a seat.

"Would you like some champagne? I have Dom."

Italy perked up, and he took her reaction as a yes.

Kenyan put the glasses and bottle on the coffee table, and sat down. "Now I know Gemini isn't the name your momma gave you, so what is your real name?"

Italy stared at him for a moment, thinking his eyes looked innocent. She liked how they dimmed inside his caramel face. Italy stirred in her seat as she stared at Kenyan's razor lined beard, inhaling his Versace cologne

"It's Italy. I normally don't tell my clients that."

"What makes me different?" he asked.

"You have an innocent look. I don't know. Maybe it's the day I'm having."

Kenyan put his arm around her.

"Do you want to talk about it? I'm a great listener."

Italy looked into his eyes.

"No, it'll work itself out," she said, sipping the champagne.

After an hour of conversation, Italy excused herself to the bathroom to change into her work clothes. She returned in a black leather thong with no top. Her fishnet stockings rose to her inner thighs while her hair and hips swayed to the Babyface song playing in the stereo.

Kenyan stood up and took his shirt off, revealing a chiseled torso.

Italy gasped, but kept it professional.

"You're beautiful," Kenyan said, pulling her into his arms.

He began kissing her neck softly, and Italy didn't resist as he cupped her ample butt into his palms, letting his fingers creep into her thong.

Italy heard all the alarms going off in her head, and pushed herself away from him.

"What are you doing? I don't allow any touching down there."

Kenyan looked confused.

"You what?" he asked, trying to grab her by the waist, as

Italy pushed him back.

"Look, Kenyan, I like you, but not that much. I came to dance. I don't mix business with pleasure."

Kenyan started to giggle.

"Dance? I called El for some pussy. I'm paying too much for a dance."

Italy's heart sank as she covered herself up and started towards the bathroom.

"I'm sorry, I didn't know that. El sent the wrong person, because I don't do that," she said, picking her clothes up off the floor.

Italy quickly put her shirt on and was about to put on the sweats when Kenyan grabbed her from behind.

"Look, I'm sorry. I thought you knew. Let's just continue our evening like we started. I know you like me."

He felt good to her. Italy began to sink into his grasp as his tongue traced along her cheekbone.

"Not like this, Kenyan. I don't even know you," she mumbled as Kenyan continued to kiss her.

"Stop," she whispered as he let his tongue slip into her ear.

Italy jerked back to her senses from the nasty feeling.

"That's enough," she said, pushing herself away from him.

"I told you I'm not like that. I don't know what you're used to, but be used to it with someone else."

Kenyans 6'4" frame towered over her as sweat dripped down his neck Italy packed the rest of her things as he stood without saying a word. The innocence faded from his eyes, and suddenly Kenyan kicked her in the back, flattening her chest into the wall. Italy tried to turn over, but met his fist as she did. Quickly, she scooted back against the wall as her mind flashed images of Donovan.

"Donovan, don't!" she yelled as Kenyan yanked her sweats off.

Italy tried hitting and kicking him, but it did nothing to

his drunken rage. Kenyan grabbed her by the thighs, pinching the meat as Italy screamed out, only to be slapped back and forth.

Kenyan flipped her over and pushed her face into the carpet as he growled and ripped off her panties. He put all his weight into the hand mashing her face. Italy squirmed left to right as Kenyan struggled to get into her pussy.

"Stop moving, bitch," he cursed as he punched the side of her head.

Italy's body lay flat from the shock of the punch, as Kenyan cussed with each thrust, harder and harder as he entered her. Italy felt the tears dripping to the carpet while her mouth stayed open, giving out soft whimpers from deep within her.

Time seemed to freeze as Kenyan continued to thrust all of his power into her while keeping her head in the carpet. Italy felt disconnected from reality as her pussy ripped at the seams. Kenyan spit on her back and choked her neck as Italy's pussy became wet and slippery, making Kenyan thrust even harder as Italy lay crippled to the situation.

"You want this cum, don't you bitch? Huh? This what you been wanting since yo' punk ass came in the room, ain't it bitch?"

With no regard, Kenyan pulled out, stood up, and ejaculated all over Italy's face and hair. Completely degraded, Italy lay paralyzed on the floor as Kenyan shook the rest of the cum that oozed from his penis onto her, and zipped his pants up. Italy rolled over as Kenyan began laughing. He reached in his pocket and pulled out the money he owed El and threw it at her as he watched her eyes: cold, solid, there, but gone. The money flew all over as Italy lay void of all reality.

"Tell El I wouldn't want to play him, so here's his doe. Paid in full! Here's an extra $200.00 for you. Now get out of here."

Italy lay still as the money stuck to her face and sweat coated body. Saying nothing as Kenyan stood over her, Italy struggled to gather the last piece of her self-respect as she balled her fists to swing at him.

Kenyan only laughed as the punch felt like a feather to a giant.

"Bitch, you got heart, I'll give you that," Kenyan said. "But I couldn't give a fuck about any of that!" he said, before kicking her in the stomach.

Italy balled into a fetal position as Kenyan wiped the sweat from his brow.

"Now get up and get the fuck out of here, before I beat the living shit out of you."

Kenyan threw Italy's clothes at her and stood over her as she struggled to get dressed. Never whispering a single threat for fear of being beaten to death, Italy found strength within herself to get her clothes on and hurry to the door. Kenyan walked closely behind, matching every step. Italy couldn't wait to feel the night's air upon her face as she approached the door while Kenyan continued to berate her and slap her on the butt until the door opened.

The cool summer breeze opened the depths of courage from within, as Italy stood in the doorway with Kenyan whispering obscenities in her ear. Suddenly, she turned around and slapped him across the face in mid-sentence. Kenyan's jaw clenched as Italy looked up into his deranged eyes.

"You gone get yours, you sick fuck you. Just remember that as you leave the house in the morning, when you start your car, and every move you make."

Kenyan laughed as he pushed her in the face then spit into her eye.

"Bitch, get the fuck out of here with that color purple shit. You couldn't do shit to me if you tried. I bet El won't even retaliate when he hears what happened. So keep it moving, bitch," he said as he kicked her away from him.

Italy stumbled back as Kenyan shut the door. Gathering herself and her dignity, she walked slowly to the car as Kenyan watched her out of the window, still laughing.

CHAPTER 4

Donovan sat outside of Uncle Roy's pool hall, contemplating his next move. Decisions raced through his head as to whom to deal with first. Gooney was easy, he thought, for he wasn't hard to find, but Italy would be a problem. Knowing Tanya told her he made bail, Donovan knew she would be hiding in the deepest crevices of the city.

He sipped from a hot bottle of Hennessey, and then threw the rest of the bottle against the curb before heading into the pool hall. The sun burned through his white tee as he looked over the cars parked in the lot. Uncle Roy's was virtually empty in the early afternoon. A few patrons hung around, conversing with the bartender while others listened to the jukebox as they shot pool.

Donovan sat at the bar looking over the thin crowd, searching for a familiar face as he ordered a Corona. After being home for two weeks, he finally decided it was time to search for Italy and finish what he started. Earlier in the day, he looked all over the city at her normal hang outs, even paying a visit to Tyrell Avenue to interrogate Italy's mother. Beth was more than willing to give up any information for a price, but even she hadn't heard from Italy in weeks.

Tyrell Avenue was busy as usual with the normal activity. Donovan took it all in as he stood on Beth's porch watching Malikie direct traffic dipping in and out of the hood, making and collecting drop offs. Thirty minutes must have passed before Beth was able to tell him to check at Uncle Roy's because Italy had been spotted there a few times that week. Donovan inhaled the information and raced so fast down the stairs that he almost tripped on a dope fiend sitting at the bottom.

"Yo, there go that nigga, Donovan," Whip said to Malikie, sitting in the seat of an old 88 Toyota Celica. "What the fuck he doing coming out of that knock bitch's spot?"

Malikie followed Donovan's every step as he hurried to his car.

"I don't know, my nigga, but you fools watch yourself out here today. Keep that heat close. I heard that nigga got knocked, but he home so he might be trying to make a run before it's all over. So you already know we ain't having that. If any of that niggas old crew even try to walk on the block, off they *on* switch, you dig?"

Whip nodded as Malikie handed him another pack to get off. Donovan noticed the two of them in the car and drove by slowly, making sure to connect eyes, leaving a stain on their unfinished business, before speeding off to the hole in the wall pool hall.

Taking small sips from the bottle of Corona, Donovan waited patiently for any signs of Italy or any of her known friends.

"Is that all you gone do is drink?" the slim bartender said as he wiped down the bar.

He tossed the rag aside, and pulled up his sagging blue Wranglers as he began sweeping the floor. With a dingy Harley Davidson t-shirt and long, dirty blonde hair, Donovan quickly took him for a hippie. He looked like Chong from the old Cheech and Chong movies.

"Is there a problem with me just sitting here and drinking a beer? I mean this is a bar, isn't it?"

"No problem at all, brother. I just remember seeing you in here a few times before. I never forget a face. I might forget your name, but I never forget a face."

Donovan smirked and took another swig from the bottle.

"Yeah, I remember you too. I'm waiting to see if someone comes through here. I had been looking for this girl for a few months. She look so good that she got me searching all over. I've seen her a few times out here and in the town, but I can't find her anymore."

"Is that right?" the bartender said as he poured a shot of whiskey. "Well, I hope you find what you are looking for. Sometimes looking for a girl you don't know could be dangerous, but good luck." The bartender slammed the shot before walking off down the bar.

Donovan turned his bottle up and left it on the counter as he made his way to the pool table.

After putting 75 cents in the machine and racking the balls, Donovan kept his eye on the open doors as he proceeded to slam all the balls into the nearest pocket. The bartender watched him as he poured shots and handed out beers, wondering what he was up to. Donovan ordered a round of shots, slamming them back to back as he played game after game of pool.

Hours passed as the liquor took its toll, leaving Donovan leaning on the bar, gripping his head. The bartender sat at the opposite end of the bar cracking jokes with the other customers about him. Hearing them, he ignored every word as he checked his watch constantly. He was beginning to see double.

"You need me to call you a cab, buddy? You don't need to be driving, and I don't need the police to know that you came from here. So stay put and I'ma call you a ride."

"Fuck that, man! I'm cool. I don't need shit but to find the bitch I'm looking for and that's it. I ain't going nowhere until she get here."

The bartender shook his head as he headed back towards the other end. Donovan checked his watch again as the door opened, letting in the bright sun light. Focusing his eyes as best as possible, Donovan cracked a smile as El and Italy walked in. They were in deep conversation as they made their way to their seats at the bar. Donovan checked his waistband as the liquor suddenly disappeared, leaving him fully alert and aware of his actions.

Italy sat with her back towards him as El rolled his eyes at her conversation.

"I don't know what type of chick you think I am, but I don't get down like that. Now if you ain't gone do nothing to that sick fucker, I'm through with this shit. Why the fuck am I working for you if I ain't protected? That's some shit I have to live with for the rest of my life."

"Let me get a Hen and Coke," El said to the bartender.

Donovan held his 45 by his side as he crawled off the bar stool. Creeping down the long counter, Donovan almost couldn't believe that Italy was sitting right in front of him, unaware of anything that was about to happen.

Italy continued talking as Donovan crept up behind her, close enough to smell the perfume coming from her neck.

El looked up as he took a sip of his drink.

"You know this nigga?" he asked Italy as he stood up.

Donovan put his hand up and exposed the pistol just enough for El to see.

"We don't need to make a scene here. This bitch was foul and she knows she got this shit coming."

Without turning around, Italy knew who was standing behind her as the voice sent chills down her spine, immediately bringing fear to the forefront.

"What you thought I would be in there forever, bitch? You thought you would get away with trying to play me? You thought you wasn't gone see me? Bitch stand up and let's go."

Italy sat paralyzed in her seat as El stepped around her.

"I don't know what you got going on with my chick, homie, but you gone have to do it moving. That punk ass pistol ain't scaring nobody either," he said, hoping that everybody watching the scene would make Donovan think twice.

Italy continued to say nothing as Donovan stood directly behind her, breathing down her neck.

"Nigga sit down before you lose your life over a bitch that ain't worth saving. Let's go, Italy."

El stepped forward, and Donovan quickly raised the gun to his face. "Nigga you think I give a fuck about these muthafuckas in here? You will die, fucking with me, cuz. The only thing I give a fuck about is torturing this bitch for the shit she did to me. So back the fuck up!"

El smiled as he stepped back. The bartender had crept up behind Donovan, quiet as a church mouse.

"Yeah, I know it's funny nigga, ain't it? I bet these bullets ain't-"

Suddenly, the bartender smashed a bottle of Grey Goose vodka over Donovan's head, grabbed the hand he was holding the gun in, and smashed it against the thick wooden counter.

The gun fell out of Donovan's hand as the bartender proceeded to twist it upward, making it feel as if it was going to snap.

El picked up the gun and tucked it in his waistband before punching Donovan in the face. Blood dripped into his eye from the gash now opened over his right eye.

Italy watching in sheer horror, but cheered as El and the frail bartender took turns beating Donovan with all they had.

Donovan accepted every hit as he kept his open eye on Italy, never breaking or blinking.

Italy smiled as they dragged Donovan through the back of the bar and tossed him in the back alley. Italy followed them and watched as he rolled over onto his knees, coughing up blood, trying his best to stop the blood from dripping into his eye.

"Come on, let's get the fuck out of here, Italy," El said, snatching Italy by the arm.

Donovan looked up one more time at the mention of her name. Their eyes locked on each other as the bartender shut and locked the door.

CHAPTER 5

Jason sat in silence as Etta James' lungs emptied into the dark cluttered room. He let his mind run in rewind as he took gulps of the Jack Daniels sitting in his lap. Sheila's face flashed over and over. Smile, flash. Her frown, flash. Feeling her kisses across his face, flash. Jason suddenly stood in front of his son, watching the incubator, thinking of his small lungs begging for air, as he lay innocent. Again, tears streamed down his face as the doctors tried pulling him off the floor, and again, the nurses holding him as Bino and Trisha pulled him to the car.

The doctors told him his wife and son were gone. Just as quickly as he had come, he was gone. While giving birth, Sheila had a placenta abruption, causing her to hemorrhage, which deprived the baby of oxygen, causing severe brain damage. For three days after the birth of his son, Jason watched the baby fight for his life in an incubator. Jason spent every waking moment with tears in his eyes as he mourned Sheila's death and prayed for his son to make it.

While watching the tiny child lay still, Jason prayed minute after minute to God, his mother or anyone who could possibly save his child. Every time the baby moved, Jason would get nervous and excited, wondering if his son was feeling all the pain he was experiencing. On day three, the doctors woke him in the waiting room to tell him that his son did not make it. All the love disappeared, as his heart poured out, soaking every inch of the room.

The funeral was small, with only five people. Jason wanted no more than that. They both were buried next to Rochelle, and he'd spent every day since, at the cemetery while his weight continued to drop.

Now, as it rained outside, Jason felt like the drops were inside of him. The tears stained the pain and questions he cursed himself with daily. Praying was useless, for he could not talk to God without any hate or disrespect for the very one who gave him life. Sheila's picture was in his hands as he slept, when he did sleep, usually, falling out in a drunken rage. Jason pulled the telephone wire from the wall and didn't bother answering the door.

"Why God, why?" he screamed, as he took another swallow of the liquor.

A knock at the door broke his thoughts. He started to answer, but couldn't gather the strength to do so. *I don't want to be bothered anyway*, he thought. The knocking continued as he stared at the door, scared to answer as he turned up the bottle once more.

"Go away," he whispered.

Becoming frustrated at the continuous knocking, Jason threw the bottle at the door, watching it burst as he opened another. Energy drained from his body with the simple thrust.

"Jason, I know you're in there. Open the door. It's Mr. and Mrs. Anderson. Open the door, Jason."

Jason sank deeper in his chair and clutched the picture of Sheila to his chest. He tucked his legs under him and began to sob softly as keys jingled in the lock. The door opened slowly as Mr. Anderson stepped in with caution. The broken bottle crunched in Jason's ear as if he were in a wide canyon, miles deep.

Mr. Anderson tried to adjust his eyes in the darkness.

Jason continued looking at the ceiling. "Get out," was all

he managed to grumble in his deep baritone. "Leave me the hell alone. The rent is in the mail."

"Jason," Mrs. Anderson whispered, not even a foot away.

Jason jumped in his seat. "Sheila?" he said, reaching his arms out, only to grab air.

Mr. Anderson turned on a light, making them all squint until their eyes became focused. Mrs. Anderson stood back and covered her mouth at the sight of Jason laying naked and sweating on the chair. Liquor bottles scattered all over the floor with turned over furniture.

"My God, son, we have to get you some help," Mr. Anderson said, turning off the stereo.

Mrs. Anderson covered him up with a quilt that had been lying on the floor. Jason shivered as she ran her hands over his head.

"Jason, honey, can you hear me?"

Jason looked at her as if he'd never seen her before. Her curly silver hair made him giggle. She smiled as he became aware of her. The alcohol oozed from his pores, making her nauseous. Mr. Anderson sat down on a stool next to the chair.

"Bobby, what do you want?" Jason asked.

Mr. Anderson smiled at the fact he hadn't lost his mind. Jason still knew who he was. "Son, we just come to check on you. Emma called and said you hadn't left the house in a few days. You have old newspapers on the porch."

"There's no reason to leave," Jason cut in.

Mrs. Anderson rose and walked to the bathroom. Jason could hear water starting to run in the bathtub.

"Emma needs to mind her damn business."

Mr. Anderson placed his hand on Jason's shoulder. "Jason, people care about you. Is that such a crime? You have to pull yourself together. Tearing yourself apart will not bring her back. Son, this might be something you don't want to hear right now, but you have to keep on living. This is not the way you honor Sheila's memory. She was a very strong woman, son, but, she was strong because you were strong."

Jason cut his eyes at him.

"Jason, death is a part of life. It's a shame her life was cut short, but you two are still connected. Her spirit is still with you, and always will be. But son, you have to pull yourself together to feel the joy of that spirit."

Jason sat up. "Bobby, hand me those pants right there, please." Jason asked, beginning to come to his senses.

Mr. Anderson handed him the sweats.

"Damn, I'm in here naked." He smiled as Mr. Anderson turned his head.

Mrs. Anderson returned to the room, wiping her hands on a towel. "Jason, sweetie, I ran you some bath water. When we leave, use it. Your shaving equipment is on the sink too."

Jason's shoulders sank. "Sheila used to do that for me all the time," he said, sitting back down slowly and putting his face in his hands.

Seeing the tears between his fingers, Mrs. Anderson sat down next to him and brought his head into her chest. Jason let it all out in the comfort of her arms. They were warm, safe, with a motherly touch that he hadn't felt in a long time.

Mrs. Anderson wrapped him tighter as his sobs became stronger. Minutes passed before Jason calmed and pulled away.

He wiped his eyes and face as she caressed his head. "Thank you," he said, standing up. "I'll be all right. I just need some more time to myself."

Mr. Anderson shook his head. "It's not that easy, Jason. As soon as we leave, you're going to go back to the same state we just found you in. You need company right now. You need to talk, and we're here to listen. Has your mother or father been here to listen?"

Jason's face became blank. "They're dead. So are Sheila's parents. There was nobody but us."

The Andersons looked at each other. Mrs. Anderson put her arm around his shoulders. "You don't have any brothers or sisters, sweetie?"

Jason became enraged at the thought of Savion. He shook

his head as he focused on the floor. “Everyone I’ve ever loved has died. My face was the first my son saw-and he died. What’s the use of keeping on, when every person I come in contact with dies? Sheila was all I had. My reason for living, and I killed her. My love killed her.”

“That’s not true,” Mr. Anderson said. “God has his reasons for everything. I know it hurts, but we have to accept it. It’s just the way it is.”

“Why Sheila, Bobby?” Jason cut in. “That was supposed to be the best day of our lives. My son, why take my son? And you tell me that’s the way things are supposed to be? God has his reasons? What the fuck? Does he have a problem with me? Since you seem to know it all, you tell me. What the fuck does God have against me? Bobby, I had to watch my wife and son die in front of me. I watched my mother deteriorate in front me from AIDS. I watched my father get shot and die in front of me. And you sit here and tell me God has his reasons? The all-loving one? He’s taken everything from me. Everything a young man needs, he’s taken, and I’m supposed to just continue my life like nothing has happened?

“Every day, I’ve been trying to understand one thing. One little thing. One question I would like answered. Why? A mother, I can understand. A father, I can understand. A wife or a son, understood. Either one, or only one, I can understand. But all of them? All of them, Bobby? One of them didn’t even get to see the world outside of a damn hospital. I held him once, Bobby. *Once*, then he was gone. I didn’t even get to kiss him. I didn’t get to tell Sheila how much I love her one last time. Bobby, do you have any idea how that feels? Can you tell me you know how it feels to have everything you love taken away?”

Mrs. Anderson released her grip as Mr. Anderson rose to his feet. She looked at her husband as he struggled to keep his tears in check. She dabbed her eye with a handkerchief while Jason opened another bottle of Jack Daniels. Mr. Anderson snatched the bottle out of his hand.

“You really want to know what it feels like to drink yourself under the table, because you blame yourself for losing someone you hold dear? Watching your wife cry every night and you being too weak to hold or comfort her because your only strength is in a damn bottle of whiskey? Do I know what you're feeling right now Jason? You bet your ass I do.

"My daughter was kidnapped when she was ten years old. Her body was beaten, raped and torn apart. Imagine the feeling of having to identify your baby girl's mutilated body. Imagine losing everything you worked hard for because you couldn't recover. Giving your life to this shit here."

Jason stared into his hurting eyes. All the joy and concern were peeled away to reveal the sadness they now showed.

Mr. Anderson held the bottle in the air. "Imagine being so afraid to have another child, that it becomes too late because you've gotten too old. Do I know what you're feeling, son? I do! That's why I'm able to comfort you, because I know what it feels like. This, what you're doing to yourself, is not the answer. This makes it worse because you dig yourself into a hole that takes years to get out of. You have to move on, son. Keep her memory dear to your heart, but you must keep living. You have to trust God's judgment. You can't blame yourself, Jason. You couldn't do anything about this situation. Life deals us so many different cards, and not all of them are good. But this is the hand we're dealt and we have to work with them."

Jason sat down on the couch as Mr. Anderson's eyes followed him.

"Jason," Mrs. Anderson said. "I loved Sheila like she was my own. We talked a lot about things. She told me about the life you two came from. I was disturbed at first, but I saw her strength, instead. I saw her fight for a better life for you, her, and that child. I wondered how someone so young, carried the spirit she had. Then I finally got a little closer to you. It was you that kept her strong. You made her think about other things than what was in front of her. She told me so. She told me you saved her, but I believe you two saved each other.

"You are complete, Jason. Every memory of her is a complete memory from a time you felt whole. Let that hold you when you feel like you can go no further. That is something no one can ever take away from you. Let those memories be your comfort. Live for both of you. After all the smoke cleared, Bobby and I saw the most important thing was that we were still breathing and we still had each other. That was something to live for. There will be many nights of tears and hurt, but let those be tears of love and strength."

Jason wiped the tears from his eyes as Mrs. Anderson rose to stand next to her husband. Jason stood and hugged them both with love and understanding flowing through the embrace.

Mrs. Anderson wiped the tears from his face. "Will you be okay tonight?"

Jason nodded his head.

"Good," she smiled. "You have two people who still love and care for you. We're here if you need us."

"Thank you," Jason whispered.

Mr. Anderson patted him on the shoulder as they began to walk out the door.

"You will be strong, Jason. Life will be good to you. Trust in the Lord."

They embraced him one more time before getting into their car.

Mrs. Anderson rolled her window down and stuck her head out. "Jason, now be strong and get cleaned up. You stink, sweetie."

Jason released a much needed laugh as they drove off.

CHAPTER 6

Weeks later, Gooney sipped a cup of coffee as he sat in his brand new H2 Hummer on Tyrell Ave., reading the Oakland tribune. A picture of Savion was plastered across the front, right next to the presidential election. Gooney looked long and hard at Savion's cold mug shot. Love and remorse was everything missing from his cold lifeless eyes. Smiling as he took another swallow from the hot Starbucks coffee, Gooney looked over everything in front of him. The block seemed empty as if everyone knew the worst was about to happen and the best thing to do was be in the house.

He folded the paper and started the car, wondering where Malikie and his crew were. The only person on the block was the youngest of them all, Sunny, looking as if he was just introduced to the life. With a harmless, more afraid than bold look, Sunny served the few fiends that scattered up and down the block. Gooney tried Malikie's phone one more time before pulling in front of the youngster.

As the voicemail clicked on, Gooney rolled his window down while pressing the end button on his phone.

"Aye, lil' nigga, who got you out here? I ain't never seen yo' scary looking ass before. Who you work for?"

Sunny paid him no attention as he continued to lean against the street sign with his hands in his pocket. The oversized white tee hung to his kneecaps, covering the sagging Girbaud jeans on top of a dingy pair of white Air Force Ones.

Gooney laughed at the youngster's sudden burst of courage. Stepping out of the truck, he grabbed a bat out of the back seat and began slapping the hollow metal against his palm as he stepped to Sunny, who watched his every move.

"So you ain't got nothing to say?" Gooney said, standing directly in front of him. "Nigga, you must don't know who the fuck I am. If you did, you would know to answer my question as soon as I asked it. Now I'ma ask you again, youngin', who you work for?"

Sunny smacked his lips as he tried to step away from the corner. Gooney stepped where he did, holding the bat out in front of him, blocking Sunny in.

"Man, watch out!" Sunny said, trying to slap the bat away. "I know who you are, so I'ma go ahead and leave. You can have this punk ass corner."

Gooney continued to block the youngster in. Quickly looking around for any lurking cop cars or under covers, Gooney pulled the bat back and thrust it into Sunny's stomach with all the power he had in him.

With the wind pulled from his body, Sunny fell to one knee as he gasped for air. He clutched his stomach and managed to whisper out a quick "fuck you" before staggering to his feet. Gooney continued to look around for cop cars or nosey people as he held the bat to his side. Kicking Sunny in the knee, Gooney laughed as the 16-year-old slumped back to the ground.

"Now I know you don't think it is going to be that easy? You just disrespected my turf, standing out here trying to sell that cheap ass dope you got, without permission. Now would you let that go down on your block?"

Gooney slammed the head of the bat into Sunny's back when he didn't answer. Sunny rolled over on the hard concrete, clutching his back as he arched forward. Gooney proceeded to kick him in the ribs as he held the bat out to his side.

"Now, I'm going to ask you one more time before I beat the shit out of you. Who the fuck you work for, or where the hell did you get the product?"

"Fuck you, Goon! I ain't telling yo' punk ass shit. Malikie and my niggas gone fuck you up for this."

"Malikie? Malikie got you out here working? Yo' little ass wouldn't know what the fuck to do in a war. What the fuck he got you out here for?"

Suddenly, a Ford Explorer screeched to a halt as Gooney stood over Sunny, demanding answers to his questions as he kicked him. Whip, Malikie and Carlos jumped out of the SUV that Fella drove.

Gooney turned around to see all of them getting out of the vehicle.

"What the fuck you got this little shit out here for?" he yelled.

Before he could say another word, Malikie punched him in the mouth with a set of brass knuckles, instantly splitting his lip. Whip looked out for the police as Gooney stumbled back. Carlos, known around the town for his quick use of a weapon immediately pulled a butterfly knife from his pocket and flung it open, slicing Gooney across the face as he kicked him to the ground. Sunny got up off the ground and began kicking him in the torso as he spit on him.

"I told you nigga," he said, stepping back.

Gooney rolled over laughing as he felt the blood rush from his face.

"You little niggas are funny. I like that rough shit, but you know all of you are dead, right? Malikie, I'ma chop yo' ass into so many little pieces, they won't be able to put you back together."

"Shut up, nigga!" Sunny said as he slapped him across the face.

Carlos pulled him back as Gooney tried to get up. Whip, quick with the trigger, pulled out his favorite Glock and slapped

Gooney across the head, opening a gash next to his ear.

"Get the fuck out of here, Sunny. We'll hit you later," Malikie said, ushering him down the street. "Get that bitch ass nigga in the truck."

Carlos and Whip pulled Gooney by his arms and stuffed him in the back seat while he continued to laugh. Carlos pulled a set of authentic handcuffs from his pocket and put them around his wrists. Gooney spit a wad of bloody mucus into his face as he snapped the rings shut.

"Muthafucka," Carlos screamed as he sliced Gooney again on the other side of his face.

Whip smacked him with the gun again, this time shattering his nose bone. Gooney screamed out in pain as Malikie got into the front seat of the truck. The tinted windows concealed everything they needed to be hidden.

"Fella, drive slow to the warehouse. We don't need to draw any attention to ourselves. Y'all stop whooping the nigga. You can do all of that when we get to the spot."

"So where the stash at, Goon? You know I know everything about you, nigga, so let's make this easy by telling me what I want to know, and I promise you will die fast. You don't, and it'll be so slow and crazy."

Gooney sat taped in a chair as Malikie stood in front of him with Whip and Carlos at the sides. The warehouse was abandoned, and so out of the way, that no one would hear him scream for miles. Gooney let his eyes take a trip around the room, somehow still thinking he would get out of it and escape.

"There ain't nowhere to go, man, you taped and we ain't letting you get away, even if you could. So where the money at, Goon?"

Gooney shook his head as the blood dripped into his lap when he bowed his head.

"Is that what this is all about?" he asked, barely audible.

"If you wanted more money, I would've given you more money, Mal."

Malikie laughed.

"Nigga please! You think I'm trying to hear that shit? You greedy nigga! You tried to eat the whole pie without giving niggas a piece. Man, you ain't fit to run the block, and it's just as simple as that. You fucked over a lot of people."

"You can't do shit without a connect. Let me get a pass, and I will bow out gracefully and get you the connect."

Malikie shook his head as he lit a Newport. "Don't need it. Your boy, Jason, got me covered. You must've done some fucked up shit to the nigga for him to basically give us the whole block for free. All I had to do was get you out the way."

Gooney's eyes lowered in sorrow, knowing Jason knew he set him up with Chico. Gooney never thought it would come back on him. He made the mistake of thinking Jason would let it all blow over. Quickly, he tried to use another route.

"Listen, the shit Jason got is garbage. He ain't gone follow through with what he say. Why you think I stopped fucking with him? That nigga is a snake!"

Carlos laughed out loud.

"Damn, nigga I never thought I'd see you begging. You think we that stupid? Big Champ is my uncle, and he and Jason's pops used to run together back in the day. My uncle told me Jay is old school solid, and I trust him before I trust yo' greedy ass."

Gooney's chin dropped to his chest. Malikie inhaled the cigarette as he watched Gooney in silence. A sad desperate man sat before him, broken, beaten, and out of options.

"What's it going to be, Goon? Looks like you all out of options. Where that doe at?"

Gooney snapped back into himself as he realized there was no way out.

"Tell my nigga Jason I love hi and I'm sorry for the plot, but it's the game. As far as my money, I got it being a stand up nigga. Giving it to you would be the weakest move ever, knowing you gone murk me. So fuck you and these peon lil' niggas you got following you. Suck my dick and get it how you live, nigga."

Malikie took one more hit of his cigarette before flicking it into Gooney's face.

"You used to be a rider, now look at you. Real niggas do real things, bitch. Y'all, off this nigga. Come on Fella, let's wait in the car."

Gooney started laughing as Malikie walked out of the room.

"It's gone be you next, nigga. That's the way the game goes, youngin'. They hate to see you rich, nigga. They hate to see you."

Gooneys words were cut off as Carlos stuck the knife through his throat, holding it there as Gooney's feet kicked out, squirming and grasping for life. Carlos twisted the knife counter clockwise as blood squirted into his face and poured down Gooney's chest onto the floor.

Whip watched as Carlos continued to twist until Gooney stopped jerking. His eyes hung open as his head tilted to the back, with the ceiling of the old rusty warehouse being his last view of life. Carlos stood back and wiped the blade of the knife off on his shirt as he looked himself over.

"Fuck, I got blood all over me, man," he said, wiping his face with his sleeve.

Whip tucked the gun back in his waistband. "Why the fuck you do that?" he asked buttoning his jacket.

"What?"

"I was going to just shoot the nigga and make it quick. You get on the crazy killer shit."

"He deserved it, though."

"I know that."

"No, I mean in life. In Puerto Rico, they say you deserved to die when you die with your eyes open. Look at his eyes."

Whip walked over to see Gooney's eyes wide open to the ceiling.

"I guess, man. All I know is you're crazy as fuck."

Carlos shrugged his shoulders as he followed Whip out of the warehouse.

CHAPTER 7

Jason drove down highway five with the radio tuned to a talk radio station. Two months had passed, but his breakdown seemed like yesterday. The steps back to normality seemed to take forever, as he finally gathered enough strength to get his mind back on track.

"Hip Hop has been a gift and a curse for the black community," spoke a listener to Joe Marshall, the creator and Dj for the very popular Sunday radio show "Street Soldiers" on KMEL.

"It has in a sense, taken young, otherwise dormant drug dealers and hustlers and turned them into millionaires. The fact that these youngsters can get into corporate America and fit right in says a lot about the mental ethics of the drug trade and what it really is, and on the flip-side, what corporate America really is. That is the gift. The curse in my opinion would be the selling out factor by steadily promoting the ills of our culture. If you aren't talking about rims, jewelry, money and half-naked women, you aren't selling any records, and that is the objective at the end of the day. It is great to see young multi-millionaires, but at what cost?"

Jason clicked the radio off and drove in silence. His hand began shaking as he pulled into the Modesto city limits. Weeks earlier, he'd driven through Oakland in search of Savion after seeing his face on the front of the Oakland Tribune. The paper also said he was wanted in connection to four murders and high volume drug sales. Jason knew that it wouldn't be long before the FBI and the DEA would be scouring the area in search of him. Jason's first thought was to leave him alone and keep his distance, but he knew Savion's days were numbered. If the Feds were on him and he was still in California, it wouldn't be long.

After checking all of Savion's local hangouts and the homes of the women that he knew, one of his baby mommas informed him that Savion had fled to Modesto and was staying with another baby momma ducking from any and every one.

West side Modesto looked similar to the fifth ward in Texas. Dirt roads and near broken down homes cluttered the area. Jason knew one thing about his brother; where ever he was, he was sure to make a name for himself. As he drove down Martin Luther King, he pulled over at a corner store to get a pack of cigarettes. Martin Luther King was like any other street in any other city named after the peaceful leader; anything but respected and peaceful. Dope dealers and junkies ran up and down the street while packs of young girls walked with their bodies hanging out of clothing, with the thugs there to greet them.

The sun shined bright, leaving the air dry and windless. Jason realized he was overdressed and took his jacket and polo shirt off to reveal his hulking frame in a tank top. Now that he was eating again, he'd started to put his weight back on.

"Mmmm," someone behind him said.

Jason turned around and gave the girl an awkward glance before walking into the store with the woman close on his heels.

"Let me get a pack of Newports and this gum," said Jason. "Hold on, let me get a bottle of orange juice."

Jason darted to the back of the store for the juice.

The woman was standing at the counter watching him as he returned. "Buy me a bottle of Henny," she said.

Jason gave the clerk a twenty-dollar bill.

"Thank you," he said, before looking the girl up and down, then walking out.

"Oh no you didn't," she said, walking quickly behind him. "Muthafucka, who do you think you are? You'll get your shit split open getting at me like that. You don't know who you're dealing with."

Jason put his bag in the car and turned to face her. He leaned on the car and let his eyes roam her body from head to toe. She was dark skinned and overweight. Her weave hung down to her shoulders in a cute design, with big, juicy lips painted with gloss, begging for a kiss. *She's a big pretty girl*, Jason thought as she pointed a finger at him while she ranted on. Jason noticed the gold and diamond rings that covered her fingers, with chains around her neck and ankles.

This is the type of girl Savion deals with, he thought.

Jason decided to humor himself and try to dig for information. "What do you want baby? I'm in a hurry."

The woman became louder and her demeanor, nastier.

"Look here," he said, cutting her off with a hardened face and lower voice.

"Number one, get your damn finger out of my face. I'm not your dude. I don't even know you. Number two, yell at your kids, baby. I'm a grown ass man. If you'd like to continue this conversation, you'd better realize it. Number three, what's your name?"

The woman caught herself, lowered her hand and softened her face.

"What's your name?" Jason repeated.

She smiled, revealing a row of the whitest teeth he had ever seen. "Sharice," she said, folding her arms over her huge breasts.

"That's better," he said, extending his hand.

"You don't know how ugly you look all frowned up. I'm Eric."

Sharice took his hand.

"Why are you so stuck up? You got a girl or something? Or you don't think I'm fine?"

Jason laughed.

"Naw, you're hella cute. No, I don't have a girlfriend. I'm just in a hurry. I'm trying to find someone."

"Who?" she said quickly.

"Damn, you got an attitude and you're nosey?"

She smiled.

"I know everyone in the West. Where are you from?"

"San Diego," Jason said.

Sharice smacked her teeth. "Damn, you come all the way up here just to see someone? It must be a bitch. Who is she?"

Jason smiled,

"She? Who said it was a she?"

Sharice dropped her arms.

"Look, it's only two things you could be doing in the West: grinding or getting some pussy. You don't look like you sell dope and you talk all proper like a white boy. So that's out. You have to be here for some pussy. You turned me down, and I'm the baddest bitch in the West. She must be a ripper because there ain't no college bitches around here. I mean ones with morals and respect for themselves like you. So you must be lost."

Jason shook his head.

"Damn, you got all of that about me that quick? Do you think you're right?"

"I'm always right, sexy. Sharice is never wrong. Ask somebody if you ain't heard of me."

Jason snapped his head back.

"So what if I talk *this way*, because I speak proper English? And what exactly does a dope dealer look like? You sound worse than white people, categorizing your own people."

"I ain't categorizing shit and you better look around you, and stop acting like you don't know."

"Anyway, how much are bricks going for out here?"

Sharice felt her eyes grow into light bulbs.

"Why you want to know? Are you the police?"

Jason laughed.

"Girl, look at me. Do I look like a fuckin' cop? Look in

my eyes."

Sharice looked and quickly looked away.

"What you turn away for?"

Sharice felt his eyes. They were eyes that she had seen before and never wanted to see again.

"So, do you want to answer my question?"

"Why is it important, Eric? Are you moving something?"

"I just want to know how much Sav is getting his off for to everyone else."

"Oh, so you're a fiend? You're one of those rich fiends."

"What?" Jason said, jerking his neck.

"You better take a look at me, not to sound conceited, but what fiend do you know look this good?"

Sharice smiled and bit her bottom lip, looking at his frame.

"That's what I thought." Jason said, jacking his slacks.

"So you're buying your shit from Sav? That nigga is a bitch." Sharice said, lighting a Newport.

"Oh, so you know him, huh? I take it that your meeting wasn't so good."

Sharice looked away from him.

Jason stepped to her and wrapped his arm around her shoulders.

"I understand. Sav don't fall in love, baby, even if she is the baddest bitch in the West."

Sharice smiled at his statement.

"Where can I find him? I didn't let him know that I was coming, this is a surprise."

"It will cost you." Sharice said, licking her lips.

"How much?" he asked, putting his hand in his pocket.

Sharice noticed it and started laughing.

"Eric, I told you I'm the baddest bitch in the West. So please believe I'm the most papered up too. I don't want yo money. You can keep your money. What I want from you is a little time and energy."

"Oh, you want me to help you move your furniture? I can

do that," he said smiling.

"Nigga, you know what I mean."

"Okay, okay I know. But I don't think you can hang with me, baby girl. Give me yo cell phone number and I will hit you after I am done handling my business with Sav."

Sharice wrote her number down as a car full of thugs rolled by, eyeing Jason.

"You think your friends will have a problem with you passing your number."

"My friends?" said Sharice, looking at the old Skylark drive by.

"Oh, them niggas ain't doing nothing. They think they hard, but they ain't shit."

The driver then threw up a turf sign with his fingers as they passed and turned a corner.

Jason took the number from her and put it in his pocket.

"What the hell was that sign? These cats banging out here?"

"It ain't nothing to worry about. You just worry about tonight and what I am going to do to you, sexy," she said, as she started to step away.

"Sharice, where can I find Sav right now?"

"Oh yeah, he will be at the park you passed down the street. He's probably on the dominos with the OGs, aiight?"

"Yeah, thanks baby, I'ma wear you out tonight," he said, as he slapped her on the butt.

Sharice giggled.

"You might want to hurry up and shake the spot. Them fool's ain't shit, but they like to try and show out. You know they all want this."

Jason laughed as he got back into his car. Sharice watched him drive off down the street. Jason threw the number out the window as he approached the park. His heart began drumming through his skin, thinking about seeing his brother for the first time in months.

What the hell am I going to say to this fool? He thought

as he parked his car.

The sun left a light burgundy stain on the sky as it descended into the other side of the world. A group of old men sat under a line of tall pine trees at a weather worn table. Jason parked his car on the street that lined the park. His mind went in a million different directions as he walked to the table. Everything around him blurred as he crossed the street.

A car horn broke his trance.

"Man, get the fuck out the street." someone yelled from the car.

Jason snapped into focus as he stared at the driver of the Skylark he had seen earlier. He counted five bodies in the car and suddenly wished he had his gun with him.

"What the fuck you looking at, nigga? Keep it moving."

Jason swallowed hard and stepped out of the car's path. The engine growled as he proceeded. Jason stared at the rusted monster as it passed.

"Damn that ain't like you, Jay. The Jason I know would have had something to say."

Jason's heart sped up as he tried to relax. Savion's voice warmed him. "I don't have my thumper, and I am out of bounds, nothing I could do."

Jason turned around to his brother's smiling face. Jason dissected his face for any resentment or anger.

"You know the only reason why they didn't get at you was because they saw me walking up."

Savion hugged him long and hard.

"So I should consider you my angel or something like that?" Jason said, as they separated.

"Naw, just know that I am good for some things you ain't."

Savion looked him over as they walked back to Jason's car.

"Nigga, you done got thin as fuck, you smoking?

Jason started laughing as they got into his car.

"Naw, just needed a change."

Savion took his hat off and rubbed his hand over his bald head. "Yeah, change is good sometimes. How'd you find me?"

Jason lit a cigarette and inhaled deeply while cutting his eyes at Savion.

"I told you that I could find you anytime I want. With your situation, I bet you tried to find me."

Savion tugged at his Rocawear sweats.

"So, is this what it's all about? You came to handle some old shit?"

Jason rolled his eyes and giggled.

"Man, you think that I will fuck with my own brother? You must be Kane, huh, to even think like that. I ain't you, man. I don't have the guts for it."

Savion relaxed in the seat at the comment.

"Why did you cut your hair?" Jason asked looking him over.

Savion lit a cigarette.

CHAPTER 8

"Shit, its real hot right now, Jay. I fucked up bad, dog. They ran my face all over the news and the paper. I'm about to move tomorrow. I don't know where I am going to go, but I got to jump."

"What did you do? I know what happened because I saw it and read it, but why?"

Savion looked at him with a distorted face. He glanced into the sky as he took a drag of the camel between his fingers.

"I fell in love."

Jason's eyes darted in every direction.

"Love, what does that mean?"

"Start the car, Jay, let's ride. I don't feel right sitting here."

Jason pulled on the freeway, heading towards his house.

"Jay don't go to the house, they watching."

"I'm not. I have something for you to see," he said, getting on the freeway.

Hours later, Jason pulled up in front of the Rolling Hills Cemetery. Nighttime choked away the day and stood over the world.

"Jay, I don't feel like standing in front of Momma's grave right now. This ain't the time, blood. The Feds are probably watching this spot too."

Jason turned the car off and got out into the cool night breeze. "Come on, Sav, this is important," Jason said, in a low, stern voice.

He zipped his leather coat up and proceeded to jump over the iron rod gates.

Savion watched him from inside the car. He inhaled his cigarette deeply and laid his head back on the seat as he exhaled. He then decided to get out the car and follow his brother. Jason stood under the thick branches of an oak tree and lit another cigarette. Savion felt a feeling of worry as he looked around.

"Jay, its hella dark out here, blood. How you know where to go?"

"I have been coming here damn near every night for the last three months."

Savion struggled to keep up with Jason as he walked briskly through the graves. He was breathing heavily as Jason stopped at the grave.

"Damn, it's cold," said Savion, rubbing his hands together as he looked around.

He paused and stared at Jason as he clicked on a flashlight. Jason took his coat off and handed it to Savion.

"Jay, what have you been coming here for the last few months for?" Savion asked.

Jason then knelt down and flashed the light on Sheila's grave.

Savion moved in closer to get a better look.

"*What the fuck?*" he said, as he stepped back.

Jason felt the tears building. Savion gathered himself and stood over Jason.

"What happened?"

Jason wiped the tears away as he tried to speak.

"Died having my baby."

"Damn." Savion whispered.

He got lost in his thoughts as he stepped back to lean on a gravestone. Jason stood up and wiped his face. Savion flicked the ashes from his cigarette as Jason stood in front of him.

"Now do you understand why I came to find you? I lost the one thing I loved more than myself. I'm not losing another one. Me and God will fight to the death before I lose another person I love, especially to the same bullshit. Sav, man you don't know the half of the shit that I have been through within this year. It started with Gooney, then you and ended with this. Naw, I'm not in my right mind. I fake it every day to keep people who care about me sane. But if you could tear open my chest, you would become intoxicated with the hurt. I had to make sure you were alive. Alive, so that I can tell you I love you nigga, and it's us through the rest of this shit."

Savion looked into his brother's eyes and saw it. The flames and the ghosts hanging from the trees in his mind screamed out at him. Savion shuddered at the stare. Jason's chest heaved up and down as he calmed himself. As his eyes watered, Jason sank into Savion's chest. They embraced, and then Jason fell to his knees. Savion pulled him back up and held him tight.

Jason's mind flashed back to the day he saw his father shot in front of him. He pulled back and turned away. Savion watched Jason look towards the sky.

"Sav, I need you, blood," Jason said.

"I needed you then and I need you now. I don't have anyone now to help me bear this shit. I tried to kill myself, man. But when I put the gun to my head, your face was the last one I saw when I closed my eyes. I have never been alone, Sav, and I am not ready to be. I had Ma and she died, had Sheila to replace her. Dead. My son? Dead. You're all that I have left. I don't give a damn about how you feel about it. I'm in your corner for it all."

Savion listened to his brother's whisper. He wiped his face and grabbed Jason by the shoulders.

"Jay, I am on the run. I don't want you to get involved in any of my shit. I am not going back to the pen, Jay."

Jason sniffed the snot back into his nose.

"Then we need to get some real money and get out of the country. As long as you stay here, you are an easy catch. Let's make them come get us. Fuck making it easy."

Savion turned to his side as he pulled his hat down tighter.

"Jay, I needed you too. I shot my girlfriend, man."

Jason stared off into the moonlight. Savion saw the distant look in his eyes as Jason lowered his head and then looked back up at him.

"Why?"

Savion fidgeted with the dirt beneath him.

"I caught her sliding wit this cat. I walk up in the bathroom at this party we were at and there she is letting him dig her from the back. The nigga started laughing like it was all good. Man, blood, I flashed so quick, I didn't know what I had done until the barrel was smoking and they were both slumped. I jumped in the car and packed my shit before the police came fuckin' with me. I had already heard that the Feds and the DEA was hanging around down there until they found me. Me and the bitch were supposed to skate, and then I find her doing that shit. Anyway, I landed in Modesto to fuck wit my boy I met in the pen, and ended up getting a little money there."

"Sav," Jason said, shaking his head.

"Why didn't you just lay low? You're attracting more heat to yourself, out there doing that shit."

"Jay, you don't think I know that I need to get out of the country? Nigga, I'm trying to get to Mexico now. I was playing a little dominos to ease my mind. A habit I picked up while in the pen."

"How much do you have stacked?"

"About five gees," Savion said.

Jason lit a cigarette as he shook his head, inhaling a long pull.

"That isn't even enough to change your whole identity. I have a pretty good amount, but we gone need more than we have put together to get there and be comfortable. Once we skate, Sav, we can't come back."

"Then we might as well tear a patch out somebody's ass

before we bail."

Jason flicked his cigarette and blew the smoke into the cold wind.

"I got an idea, but we have to be real slick."

"Whatever it is, I'm wit it." Savion said.

Jason knelt down and kissed both of the gravestones. He ran his fingers over Sheila's name. The name carved in the marble read 'Sheila Wright.'

"Y'all got married?" Savion asked, after reading the inscription.

Jason ran his finger across the picture of her and then put his coat back on and zipped it to the top.

"We were supposed to this year, but that was my wife even without the paper," Jason said as he lit another cigarette and walked back to the car.

CHAPTER 9

Beth woke up from a long alcohol driven night in a cold sweat. Morris, her cocaine buddy lay knocked out next to her in a dream. Beth looked around the room at all the clothes scattered across the floor. Pulling back the covers, Beth saw that Morris was buck-naked. Suddenly, she began shaking her head as the reality pounded her brain. Quickly, she got up and scoured the room, searching for a condom wrapper or signs of one being used. Morris was also a heroin addict and on more than one occasion, she'd witnessed him sharing needles with other junkies.

"No, no, no," she screamed as she tossed over clothes and pillows as the search became frantic.

Morris awoke, smiling as he watched her bubble butt jiggle as she moved.

"What you looking for, Beth?" he said as he scratched his uncombed nappy hair.

Beth ignored him as she dumped the bedroom wastebasket onto the floor. Getting down on her hands and knees, she picked through the trash, praying she would find a wrapper, or the condom itself.

"Damn, you lost some work or something?" Morris said as he stood up, scratching his stomach.

"It's early as fuck, but a nice hit would be cool right now to start the day."

"Shit, shit, shit," Beth screamed out as she held her head in her hands.

Morris stroked his long dirty dick until it got hard and stood over her as she knelt down on the floor.

"Whatever is wrong, this should make you happy, baby girl. You screamed out to God last night when I put this fat dick in you. Gone and lick it again and make everything better. I got some money for a hit after I rip that pussy up again."

Beth took her hands from across her face and looked up at him as his dick rested on her forehead. Morris looked down, smiling as he stroked the side of her face. Beth saw nothing but the hair surrounding his balls and butt crack and quickly became disgusted with the very thing she'd loved just hours prior.

Morris held his hard dark dick in his hands and began slapping it back and forth between her forehead and cheek. Beth sat in silence through the humiliation as she thought about the virus eating away at her blood cells at that very moment.

"Come on baby, suck it like you did last night," Morris said, continuing to smile at her.

Beth looked down at the floor as she thought about her life being over. Hearing nothing but Morris laugh at her and the moment did nothing but pour gas over the fire.

Without warning, Beth grabbed his balls and yanked them with all her might. Morris screamed out in pain as he stumbled forward, trying to grab at the soreness. Beth jumped to her feet as he fell to the floor, screaming in agony. Putting on her tennis shoes, she ran and cocked her leg back and swung it with everything she could muster, slamming into his hand. Morris let his balls go and now held his hand with the other.

"What the fuck is wrong with you?" he screamed out as Beth stood over him.

"You nasty fucker, you fucked me without a condom? You know I was drunk as shit last night, and you let that go down? Everybody knows you got that sauce, muthafucka!"

Without hesitation, Beth kicked Morris in the balls again. This time, with all foot and force, connecting head on. Morris screamed out again and tried to curl up, but Beth was quicker as she continued to kick him in the same place repeatedly. Morris felt as if he was going to die as his eyes rolled back in his head. After about fifteen kicks, Beth stood back and looked down at his seemingly unconscious body. Morris began to try and crawl his way to standing up. Beth stood back as she watched him.

"Now get your shit and get the fuck out of here!" she screamed at the top of her lungs.

Morris got to his feet and tried stumbling over to her. Beth ran out of the room and grabbed one of the guns Malikie and his crew left over there in case of a war. Checking to make sure it was loaded, she ran back in the hallway as Morris leaned against the doorframe holding onto his balls for dear life. Beth held the gun at her side.

"What you think you bout' to do, you dirty dick mutha-fucka? I said get the fuck out and you better do just that."

Morris looked up at her holding the gun in her hand.

"What, you gone shoot me? You think I give a fuck about that? I'm already dead, bitch. Yeah, I got the sauce. You the dumb bitch that wanted to fuck me. You were so concerned about this dick. You want to be mad at somebody, be mad at yourself. I'ma leave with no problem."

Beth felt the tears run down her face as he turned to go back in the room. Trembling in place, she clutched the gun closer to her as she slowly walked to the open doorway. Morris slowly put his dirty ragged clothes on as he struggled to stay on his feet. Beth watched him move, thinking that he fucked her with no condom on purpose to give her the virus. Unconsciously, Beth cocked the hammer back on the 45 and pointed it at him as he dressed.

"You dirty dick fucker." she whispered loud enough for him to hear.

Morris smacked his lips while turning around to face her.

"You can be mad all you want to and call me what you

want to, but the bottom line is you wanted the dick and you got what came along with it. I think you have more important shit to deal with now, other than me."

Beth looked at the floor in a trance. Death seemed to be the only thought that crossed her mind. Consumed with rage blended with guilt, Beth raised the gun to Morris while still looking at the floor. The barrel lined up with his left cheek.

"So what you gone kill me, Beth? Well here I am. Do what you gotta do," Morris screamed out with his arms raised to the ceiling.

Beth blankly stared at Morris without saying a word.

"That's what I thought," Morris said, attempting to brush past her.

Without a second thought, Beth squeezed the trigger, releasing two shots that slammed into Morris's left cheek, ripping through his jawbone and tearing the left side of his face off. Morris flew back into the blinds and bounced forward onto the bed. Beth fired one more shot into his forehead as she stood over him, watching the smoke from the hot bullet chill in his head. Still in a trance, she dropped the gun and slid down the wall onto the floor, staring at the dead body in her bed. The sunlight peeked through the dark room, reflecting light on the chrome pistol.

Hearing the shots from the block, Malikie quickly ducked down in case someone was firing at him.

"Where the fuck that come from?" he asked Whip, who was already laying on the floor, gun in hand.

"I don't know, but it was close. We need to go upstairs and get some more heat just in case."

Malikie nodded as he slowly rose to his feet. Whip got up and dusted his clothes off as he looked around. Tucking the gun back in his waistband, he and Malikie walked across the street timidly as they surveyed the scene. The rest of the workers came out of their safety zones, looking up and down the block. Malikie quickly stepped into the room and rushed to his gun stash. Whip closed the door behind him, looking around the room.

"Where the old broad at? She normally up by now, waiting for a free hit."

Malikie looked towards the back of the house as he dug around for his favorite 45.

"Whip, you got my .45, blood?"

"Naw, it was in there last night. You know I stay with the Glock."

Malikie stood up and looked around the room.

"That don't make no sense. I know it was here. Let me see if this bitch awake."

Malikie rushed to the back of the apartment, looking in every room until he got to Beth's. He stopped when he entered and paused at the sight of his 45 on the floor and Beth sitting against the wall, still dazed from what had happened. Malikie walked over to the bed in shock as he stared at Morris' stiff, dead body. Glancing back at Beth still staring at the floor, Malikie picked his gun up off the floor and tucked it in his waistband.

"I done seen too much death happen in these last few months. What the fuck happened here?"

Beth continued to stare at the floor in silence. Malikie stood over her, watching.

"Auntie? Auntie, what the hell happened?"

Beth snapped out of her trance.

"He killed me, nephew. I need to find my daughter."

"What you mean he killed you?" Malikie asked as Whip walked into the room.

"What the fuck happened in here?"

"I'm trying to find out right now."

"He killed me, nephew. That dirty dick muthafucka gave me that virus. I got to find my daughter before they put me in jail."

Malikie stood back from her as if she was now somehow contagious. Whip stared at the dead body in silence, focusing on the single shot to his head.

"Yo' she a good shot, my nigga. That shit look real professional."

"Shut up nigga! This ain't the time for that."

Malikie stared down at Beth in silence. Being that he was now the boss, he knew he had to have the love of the hood in order to stay in power. Plus, Beth had looked out for him and his whole crew whenever he needed her. Malikie wasn't the one to turn his back on good people regardless of who they are and what they do.

"Yo' Auntie, I need you to get up and get some clothes on. I'ma get you out of here and take care of all this shit. Right now, you got to get out of here, though."

Beth looked at him with the glassiest eyes as he knelt down in front of her.

"Thank you, nephew. I have to find my daughter though. Can you help me with that?"

Malikie nodded as he helped her up off the floor.

"Get dressed, and I'ma have my boy take you to a hotel. We gone find Italy for you."

Beth covered her body with her hands as she walked out of the room. Whip watched her as she slowly walked passed.

"Why you helping that knock bitch? Don't nobody give a fuck what she got. All she gone do is go out there and give it to another knock."

Malikie looked back at the dead body lying across the bed.

"Gotta take care of the hood, my nigga. That's how they love you, when you show love back. This our turf, and being that, we gotta take everything that goes wrong and fix it. That way, the people respect us instead of fear us. I don't want anyone to fear us to the point they bring the boys around. It's bad enough they already here and they already scared to death anyway. We gotta be old school with the way we run this, you dig? If the people have a problem, they can come to us with it and we'll take care of it. So right now, I want you and Fella to take this body to the warehouse and burn it. Carlos and I are gonna get her to a hotel."

Whip nodded as he put on his burners. Malikie opened

his phone and called the rest of the crew.

"Y'all come upstairs," he said, before hanging up.

"Y'all make sure you keep those gloves on too. Try to get a line on that pretty light-skinned girl we used to be on. The one with the long legs. That's Auntie's daughter, Italy."

CHAPTER 10

"Jason, Jason is that you?" a soft feminine voice asked behind him.

Jason turned around in surprise, as he looked down at Christian, Gooney's old love. Beautiful, with a serious, but carefree look, Jason took in all of her caramel glory. Everything inside South Land Mall became quiet and distant as an unexplainable feeling came over him. He suddenly wanted to put the Jordans he was holding down and replace them with her.

"Christian," Jason said with a smile. "How you been doing?"

Christian ran a hand through her long burgundy and brown dreads. Jason sank into her hazel eyes as she spoke with force and confidence.

"Everything is good with me. Just picking up the pieces of a few things since Goon is gone, but nonetheless, I'm good. Where have you been? I haven't seen you in school in a minute."

Jason glanced away, unable to shake his smile.

"Yeah, I know I been slipping on that. I just have been having a lot on my plate. I heard about what happened to Goon. I heard they found him in a warehouse, stabbed up."

"Yeah, everything finally caught up to him. That was one of the reasons I couldn't stay with him. Why weren't you at the funeral? I was looking for you, hoping we could talk over a cup of coffee. I heard what happened to Sheila."

Jason cringed at the mention of his beloved's name.

"I was so tired of funerals and death. Plus, me and Goon fell out really bad before he died. Not that I wish death on anyone, but I just couldn't do it."

"What did you two beef about?

"Power and money! You know how Goon got really big headed?"

"That I do know like I know myself. You were always the smart one. To tell the truth, I wanted to be with you for so long. Goon was charming, but you had that mystery about you that was hard to resist. But I had so much respect and admiration for you and Sheila's relationship that I just kept it to myself and watched from the side."

Jason was shocked as he took her hands in his.

"I don't know what to say right now. I'm in shock more than anything. Why tell me now?"

Christian smiled as she stepped in closer.

"Well, you are free by unfortunate circumstances, but you are free. I don't want to miss my chance, Jason. You are still very much a good man, and I know you aren't in the life anymore. I'm attracted to that. Every day at school, I wanted to tell you. But like I said, I had to have respect."

Jason nodded as he continued to hold her hands.

"Well, I appreciate your morals. Maybe we can try something. I can't lie and say that I ain't feeling you right now, 'cause I am. I just have a lot on my plate that I have to deal with."

"I understand to the fullest, Jay. Just give me call when you have a chance. I won't force anything. If something is meant to be, it will be."

Jason loved her frame of mind and the way she thought. He squeezed her hands in his as he smiled in silence.

"So what is it going to be Mr. Wright? Will we be able to talk after this?"

Jason nodded his head as he stared at her full, pearly

white smile.

Christian shook her head as she held his stare.

"I see this is going to be harder than it looks trying to get into you."

"That's right girl, bend that ass over for me. Let me see it jiggle."

Italy complied with the horny customer's wishes as she gave him a wall dance. His palms felt like sweaty mittens as he rubbed them up and down her thighs while his fat stomach grinded against her backside as she pushed herself into him. The cigarette and alcohol smell seeped from his pores and breath, as he whispered into her ears.

Italy jumped back at the razor sharp stubble of his jaw, as it scratched her neck.

"I never met a black bitch like you. Grind harder, baby."

Italy turned him out as she grinded against his belly harder. She stood nude while the man fondled her with his sweaty palms, one gripping a breast and the other between her legs.

"Your titties are so full and plump. I will give you an extra $20 dollars to let me suck one."

He then reached into his pocket, pulled the money out, and held it in front of her face. Italy took the money and turned around as he began to lick and play with her nipples.

She grimaced at his double chin and chapped lips as he drooled all over her breasts.

"Hurry up, baby," she said, while playing with the other breast herself.

The pudgy man licked and began, once again, sucking on her protruding nipples.

"I see that I have gotten you hot," he said between sucks.

Italy fake-panted as the man got sloppy and rough.

"You like that?" The man said, as he stuck his hand between her legs again.

"No, no," she said, removing his hand. "That will cost you again."

He dug in his pocket and pulled out a bunch of paper and lint.

"Damn baby, I don't have any more money. Let me just get jacked off until the next time."

Italy put her robe back on and stuck the money in her pocket.

"I will see you next week, Walter. You know the rules."

"You're right," he said, as he grabbed his coat.

"I have to get home to my wife. Until next time, Gemini."

Italy sighed as she walked into the dressing room to count her money.

"What up, LeeLee? You phat tonight?"

Italy looked up to see who was talking to her.

"Damn Denise, is your ass getting bigger?" Italy said with her eyes fixed on the dark skinned woman's butt.

Denise stood a mere 5'2" with most of her weight in her butt. Her breasts were small and her hair was cut close to her head. The green contacts and blonde hair dye made her look tacky, diminishing her natural beauty, but Denise was gay and always hit on the new girls in the club.

"I don't know," Denise replied. "Why don't you come over here and hold it for me."

"No thanks," Italy said, as she continued to count her money.

"$500. Cool," she said, as she began changing her clothes.

"Hey LeeLee, do you want to go to this party with me tonight?" Denise asked.

Italy began laughing as she pulled her Seven jeans up.

"With you, naw I'm cool. Any party that you're going to doesn't have men. Plus, I don't swing that way."

Denise shut her locker and stood in front of Italy and began running her fingertips in circles down Italy's arm.

"That ain't what your eyes say. And as a matter of fact,

it's not what your body is saying right now."

Italy's body melted at her touch, feeling paralyzed by her power. "That's what I thought, I can take that pussy right now, but I will wait until you give it to me."

Italy then snapped back into focus and pulled her arm away.

"Yeah right, bitch," she said, laughing.

"I'll see you later," Denise hollered as she walked out of the room.

Minutes later, the door flew open as Italy began to walk out.

"Move bitch," said Chandra as she stormed into the room.

Italy almost stumbled when she bumped her way past.

"Excuse you!"

Chandra threw her purse down and quickly took her coat off.

"What did you say you ugly ass bitch? I know you ain't back talking anyone. Don't fuck around and get your pussy took, like my nigga Kenyan did. Shit, Denise has wanted to hit it for a minute. I'll fuck you up and let her get you."

Italy lowered her head and walked out of the room as she began laughing.

"Ha-ha, that's what I thought, bitch. Do it moving."

Italy continued out the door as she flipped her off, shuddering at the thought of Kenyan and everything that happened that night. She never called the police or pursued the subject, and El only said he'd take care of it when she told him.

Chandra was Kenyan's cousin and best friend, so after that night, Kenyan had come to the club and harassed her when he saw her. Chandra was 5'7" and overweight. Her belly stuck out way further than her breasts, and she had no butt to shake, leaving her to do other things in the club. With pale caramel skin and a busted weave that was seldom done, Italy had caught her on numerous occasions doing "extras" for her clients.

Italy pulled her hood over her head and gripped her purse

close to her side as she started walking to the Bart. The San Francisco breeze stung her cheeks and made her eyes water as she made her way down Market Street. She noticed that the Cineplex was starting to fill up as she left. More men hurried past her with their heads hung low. She thought of going back to make a couple hundred more, but suddenly realized how tired she was and continued on to the station. The foul stench of urine and garbage made her stomach turn as she fought to hold her breath. She gagged while walking down the stairs of the Seventh Street station.

The station was nearly empty as she hurried to catch the last train. "Damn, I need to get a car, *for real*," she mumbled to herself as she boarded the train to Oakland.

The train car was empty except for one other person. She took the furthest seat away from him and studied the back of his head. The glare from the lights reflected off his dark shaven head. Italy noticed how smooth it was. The hulking shoulders he possessed made her wonder what he might look like.

Her mind drifted back to the comment that Chandra had made to her before leaving the club. She ran a mental marathon through her life as the train thundered through the tunnels under the city. Italy wondered how her mother was doing and tried to dismiss the thought before it got too deep.

She closed her eyes and caught an image of Jason's smile the first time they had met. The thought of feeling Donavan's foot against her skull came at that moment and made her head begin to throb as she wondered just how hard he was looking for her.

As she opened her eyes, she noticed the man's frame turned to the side and him stretching his legs out, clutching a book in his hand. Italy noticed that he kept his focus to his lap and then heard a clicking sound and realized it was coming from a laptop. The stern look on his face made her smile as she studied Jason's face. Her heart began to beat out of her skin as butterflies mated in her stomach. She twisted her body in her seat as the nervousness controlled her. She wanted so badly to call his name, but choked the words before they could escape.

Jason looked back at her, coughed and then turned back to his book. He quickly frowned as he turned around to take another look at Italy's now reddened face.

He squinted beneath his glasses as he sat the book down to get a better look.

"Italy?" he said, as the train stopped at Embarcadero Station.

Italy put her hand up as she swallowed and struggled for air. She wiped her eyes and stood up to walk to him. Jason noticed she'd put on a few extra pounds in the right areas as she approached. He put his laptop in the seat next to him and stood to give her a hug. Italy melted into his warm chest as he squeezed her into him.

Jason released his grip and looked into her face as he sat down.

"It's been rough, huh?" he said, saving the material on the screen.

"What makes you say that?" Italy said sitting down across from him.

"Your eyes say it all. You know you're an open book to anyone who pays attention."

Italy shook her head. "You still haven't shaken that attitude, huh?"

Jason smiled.

"That's not having an attitude. That's just being attentive," he said, putting his things into his backpack.

The train jerked to a stop.

"This is why I don't like taking the Bart. You know we're under the water right now?"

"So there is something Jason is afraid of. I thought that mug of yours was fearless."

Jason smiled as he glanced at her lips.

"So how have you been doing?"

Italy sighed as she looked out into the darkness of the tunnel.

"I'm surviving. That's all I can demand of myself right now. Just survive through all the bullshit."

"So how much bullshit has there been?"

"So you care again?"

"Never stopped. You chased me away."

"Did you ever wonder why?"

"For a minute, but it passed. I understood."

"Understood what?" Italy said.

"I understood that you liked me."

"You are sure of yourself, huh?"

"No, just very attentive," Jason said with a smile.

"What makes you think that I like you?"

"I said *liked*, but you know what you feel, right?"

Italy rolled her eyes as she giggled.

"You have quick answers. Do you think before you speak?"

"Not when I know what I'm talking about. I think you just listen too slowly."

Jason rubbed his hand over his goatee as Italy stared out into the night's darkness.

"Why so nervous?" she asked.

"I'm not nervous. My mind moves too fast, so when I'm still, I have to play with something."

"What are you doing on the Bart? What happened to your car?"

"It's at the station I'm getting off at."

"How's Sheila?"

Jason stopped his movements and reached for his pack of cigarettes.

"That's a nasty habit," Italy said, covering her mouth.

"So is life, but we have to live it. I have to have something to calm my nerves."

"Why are your nerves rattled? I don't know you that well, but I do know your nerves don't get rattled."

Jason smiled at the comment. He exhaled and blew the smoke to the ceiling. "What's going on with your fast ass friend?"

"Who, Tanya? She's anything but fast anymore. I think what happened between me and Donovan really shook her up. She got into nursing school and is about to graduate. We really don't talk much anymore. You know how it is when two people are going in different directions?

"You sound more mature."

"Living life and going through it will do that to you."

"Did you ever read those books I gave you?"

"No, I didn't. I don't have the time."

"You have nothing but time now."

"I have too much on my mind. My life is a book."

"So, how do you like stripping?"

"How did you know I was dancing?"

"Let's just say, I keep my ear to the street."

"So you out asking about me?"

"No, people just run their mouth. I heard about that incident with Donovan at the bar."

The train stopped at Fruitvale Station. Jason grabbed his things.

"It was good seeing you again. Stay out of trouble."

"Jason," Italy said, rushing behind him.

"Would you mind giving me a ride home?"

Jason looked at her for a second as they stepped off the train.

"I guess I have to now, huh?"

Italy bit her bottom lip as she grinned. She leaned in to give him a kiss, but stopped before their noses could touch. Jason didn't pull back. Italy was shocked as she stepped back.

"Jason, you were going to let me kiss you?"

Jason exhaled the fog out of his mouth as he looked at her and then the other side of the station.

"It's been a while since I've been kissed. I miss what it feels like."

Italy stared at him, speechless, as he looked at everything except her. He patted her arm and began walking to the stairs.

Italy followed behind him in silence as they walked to the car.

"Damn Jason," she said, once inside.

"I thought about this car a million times. I remember hoping that I would see it, and you, again. Jason, you never answered my question?"

"What's that?" he said, letting the car warm up.

"What's up with Sheila?"

Jason bowed his head and stared at his lap as he played with his fingers.

"She passed away," he said, as he turned the volume up to a Maxwell CD left in his deck.

Italy saw that he was bothered by the thought and left it alone. Jason glanced at her out of the corner of his eye. Italy watched the road as she felt his stare stain her face as "This Woman's Work" squeezed through the silence.

"Sometimes, things are hard to understand," said Jason.

"The things you don't get, seem to play over and over in your head. You go through every emotion you can possibly think of, from blaming yourself to cursing the heavens above. In the end, you realize it wasn't meant for you to understand at that time, but one day, it will all make sense. Do you get what I'm saying?"

Italy nodded her head as Jason pulled into a Safeway parking lot.

"Some of the things I've been going thru are unexplainable, but I get it."

"You should get it, because it's self-inflicted. You put yourself through the same things that you had already been through, from the first time I met you."

"Why are you raising your voice at me? Your pain is not my fault."

"You're right, it isn't. But you expect me to feel sorry for you, well I don't. Every… or shall I say *almost* every situation you get into is because you have brought it on yourself to go through that pain. It's easy to blame someone else, isn't it? But the bottom line is no one will love you or look out for you better than yourself."

"So are you saying I don't love myself?"

"What do you spend your money on?"

"That's none of your damn business what I do with my money."

"I can tell you without you even saying a word, and that's weed and clothes. Am I right or wrong? In fact you don't even have to answer that, because I know that I am right."

Jason got out of the car and walked briskly into the store. Italy gritted her teeth and banged her hand on the dashboard. She then got out and ran after him. Jason stood in front of the produce section, trying to decide what brand of orange juice to get.

"So why do you care, Jason? This is my life, and I can do as I choose. If that's what I want to do, then that's my business and problem."

"You're right," he said, as he put a bottle of Tropicana into his basket. He then proceeded on to the bread section.

"Then why did you jump down my back? One minute things are all good and the next, you are flipping."

"My bad," he said, grabbing a couple loaves of bread.

He went on to the frozen food section and grabbed a variety of ice cream.

"Do you think that it's easy being me and doing what I do, Jason? Walk a day in my shoes and let me know."

"I never said that it was. I said you make it hard for yourself with everything against you already. It makes no sense, if you ask me."

"Why do you think that you know everything? You think you are perfect."

Jason laughed as he pushed the cart to the checkout counter.

"I don't think that I know everything, Italy. It is just common sense and plain logic. You want to be noticed in the mix of the hype. So you are doing anything and whatever to get it. But your love for the hype will kill your natural love."

The cashier nodded her head in agreement, as Jason paid

for his groceries.

"Listen to him, girl. I have been there. The Lord knows I have."

Italy rolled her eyes at the woman and followed Jason out of the store.

"Well, if I am so wrong, then why don't you show me the way? You act like you care."

Jason put his groceries in his trunk and opened his door.

"Why are you so busy trying to be in my life every time we bump into each other? Instead of trying to be my broad, why don't you just listen? Is that so hard? You've tried your way over and over, try a new way. I don't want you as my woman. I don't mess with strippers. You have a lot to swallow in order to get where you need to be. Do you think anything worth having comes overnight?"

"*Stripper?*" Italy yelled, slamming the door.

"Nigga, you don't have any right calling me that. Just because I do what I have to do to survive, doesn't mean you can judge me. You sell dope, Jason. If you were a female, you'd probably be in my position too. Don't take your anger out on me. I don't deserve it. I haven't tried to do anything but be your friend. Do I feel something deeper for you? Yes! I never had a man care about me before. The things you have told me, I think about and actually try to carry out, but reality is cold when I step outside of this car."

Jason sped onto the freeway and put his Lauryn Hill CD into the deck. For minutes, they rode in silence. Jason put a cigarette in his mouth as he thought about everything that was said.

He cut his eyes back and forth at Italy as she stared out of the window.

"You're beautiful, Italy," he said, lighting his cigarette.

"Too beautiful to be going through the things you are."

Italy smiled. She let her window down and snatched the cigarette from his lips and tossed it to the wind.

"That's a pet peeve of mine. I hate cigarettes. Please wait until I'm gone to smoke."

Jason laughed as he turned the music down.

"You should be in a position of control. Beautiful smart women are dangerous, but only if they know their own power. Most women don't even realize that they don't have to fuck their way to the top. That's just the easiest way there. But you have to see this; when that man gets tired of the sex you give him, you become another face. Nothing more! Now play the power card, and respect is automatically given. There might be a little hate behind it, but if you are on top of your plan, you'd already know that.

"That's the reason I ride you every time I see you. You're too beautiful for this. You're higher than this. I knew it the first time we met. You're fearless. That's the first step to taking on the world. No fear! What is something you've always seen yourself doing?"

Italy shrugged.

"I don't know. I've always wanted to be a fashion designer."

"Then why don't you go to school for it? Women are hustlers too. The key to hustling is to keep your money flipping. Never let it rest. Always flip it into something lucrative. Set a goal for yourself. Nothing big, but something very reachable. That way, the small ones turn into big ones. That's what me and Sheila used to do. We always made our goals happen. But it's all in what you want. If you want that street fame, don't complain about what comes along with it. The world will dish out all kinds of pain. It's all in which world you chose."

Italy let her seat down and stared at the ceiling.

"Some things you just can't escape, Jason. If it could all be as simple as you make it, the world wouldn't be the way it is. You still sell dope to survive, and you're one of the smartest people I know."

"I don't deal anymore. Sheila and I got to where we wanted to be before she passed. I'm working on something else now."

"What is that?"

"I'm writing a book, or trying, I should say. Every time I sit down to do it, something pops up."

"What is it about?"

Jason smirked.

"What do you think?"

"I don't know, maybe your life?"

"Naw, that's too easy. It wouldn't be a challenge."

"Then what?"

"A young girl's struggle. Basically, my mom's."

"Whoa! Is that easy?"

"No! I have to bring up a lot of things I buried a long time ago. Italy, I know firsthand what you are going through. I'm not going to speak on it anymore. I think I've said enough."

"Well do you think there's any chance we can just smile together? Get off at High street."

Jason sped the car up as they continued to talk.

"I don't know. I'm real busy, and I'm sure you are too."

"Jason, why won't you accept me when I offer? You're not even with Sheila anymore and you still deny me when I offer. Yet, you sit here and tell me how beautiful and smart I am?"

Jason got off the freeway at High St.

"Which way do I go?"

"Make a right on East 14th." Italy said as she dreaded going back to El's house and having to deal with Bianca and her mood swings.

"I stay on 51st and East 14th."

Jason shook his head as he smiled.

"Damn, you stay right on the track, huh?"

"Ain't that something?" she said as she thought about the night El sent her to Kenyan.

Jason made a right turn onto the dark, barely lit street.

"I stay right in that third house. You can let me out right here if you want," Italy said as she looked at all of the lights still on in the house.

Jason noticed a Navigator and BMW parked in front of

the house.

"Nice cars, but he has you walking and catching the Bart all over the place? That can't be love."

"It's not love at all, it's all business. That's all this business is. Good night, Jason."

Jason nodded his head at her as she stepped out of the car.

Italy noticed Bianca staring at her out of the window as she watched Jason's car drive off. Italy waited until his lights disappeared before she began up the stairs.

CHAPTER 11

Out of nowhere, Donovan came from behind a car and slammed his fist into Italy's jaw, knocking her on the hood of the BMW. Italy rolled over the custom hood and fell unto the concrete, once again at the mercy of Donovan's foot. Bianca and El stood at the window watching the horror as Donovan proceeded to rip and pull all of Italy's clothes off her, at the same time he kicked and punched at her body.

"That's a little bit too much, Bianca. That nigga is going crazy." El said as he took a sip from a bottle of Pepsi.

Bianca, who had become very envious of Italy and all the attention she received, had run into Donovan earlier in the day at Durant square, a local flea market of sorts. Knowing Donovan since high school, Bianca quickly got into his business and was shocked to hear about the history of him and Italy. After telling him she knew were Italy was, Bianca rushed home to alert El that Italy was a scam artist and was probably thinking of setting him up any day.

Bianca invited Donovan over and he and El discussed everything that had happened between the two of them. El, never the one to violate the game, gave Donovan his blessing to do what he wanted with Italy. He felt that anyone who crossed over should be dealt with for biting the hand that fed them.

Donovan pulled Italy by the hair as she kicked and screamed as loud as she could, hoping someone would hear her and call the police. Through it all, Italy glanced up to see Bianca smiling as El watched in silence.

"Bitch, I told you I would find you wherever you went. Even yo' pimp ain't feeling yo' set up ass. Now you gone get everything you deserve."

Donovan backhanded Italy, immediately splitting her lip. Still holding onto a patch of her hair, Donovan opened the door to his BMW and tossed her in the front seat. Italy lay in shock and pain, holding her face in her hand as she gripped her stomach with the other. Donovan looked up at El and Bianca still standing in the window and nodded his head as he got into the driver side of the car.

Both of them watched as Donovan continued to smack and punch her as he started the car. Italy glanced up at El and Bianca once more as Donovan peeled away from the curb.

"Whewww! You don't know how good this feels right now. I'm 'bout to do some serious torture shit to you, bitch. You just don't know. You fucked over the wrong nigga. You hear me, bitch?" Donovan screamed as he slapped her once more before shifting gears.

Italy cried and watched East 14th fly by her as she looked out the window, thinking this would be her last time seeing any of it. Donovan shifted gears again as he picked up the speed to 110 mph down the somewhat empty boulevard.

"I know you thought you wasn't gone never see me again, huh? I know bitch, I know. Don't worry, I might get so caught up in the moment that I end it quick, so pray for that instead of your life."

Donovan slowed down as a cop car pulled out into traffic in front of him, moving at a snail's pace. Italy saw this as her only chance to escape. Donovan paid her no attention as she quickly put her hand on the door handle and swung it open.

"What the fuck?" he yelled in surprise as he hit the

brakes while Italy dove out of the car onto the pavement.

"This bitch just keeps trying me!" He said to himself as he got out of the car.

Feeling as if all her bones had just cracked, Italy jumped to her feet and ran down the boulevard, naked, screaming for her life.

The cop car slowed to a stop and reversed as Donovan jumped in his BMW and punched the gas until he was flying by. The cop got out of the car as Italy hobbled up to him screaming at the top of her lungs.

"He's trying to kill me again," she said, jumping into the cop's arms.

"Who?" he said, trying to calm her.

"Donovan! He's already on bail for trying to kill me before, and now he's trying again."

The cop opened the back door for Italy and sat her down before picking up his radio and giving a description of the car.

"Just please catch him," Italy whined.

"He keeps finding me, and all I'm trying to do is live my life!"

The cop opened his trunk and got her a blanket as she sat in the back of his car, trembling from the cold.

Donovan kept his eyes in the rearview as he punched the gas down East 14th. Swerving, he made a right on 73rd and punched it down the long street, trying to make his way to the freeway. Two cop cars in the area got the call and jumped on his tail as he sped by them. Donovan jumped in his seat at the sight of the flashing lights.

"I ain't going back again over this bitch!" he screamed as he switched gears again, speeding up even more.

Seeing the San Jose freeway ramp, Donovan tried to slow his speed to hang with the curve of the road. Slamming on the brakes as the car fishtailed, Donovan lost control of the small BMW and spun wildly into the side embankment, smashing the side of the car, then bouncing back into oncoming traffic. The cop cars stopped, and quickly pulled their pistols as they approached the hunk of metal reduced to scraps.

Pieces of the hood and headlights crunched under their feet as they attempted to open the driver's side door. Donovan lay still, not moving a muscle as the cops pulled at the door.

Finally getting it open, the cops pulled his body from the car and quickly began kicking and punching him; something police officers normally did to high speeders trying to evade the law. Donovan lay stiff on the concrete, still not moving.

"Check his pulse," one of the cops said. "He ain't even moving!"

One of the cops knelt down and put his finger to Donovan's neck, feeling around for any sign of life. Checking and rechecking, the cop found nothing.

"He's dead. There ain't no sign of life coming from this boy at all."

Italy sat in the back seat as the cop that saved her life pulled up to the scene and ran to where Donovan laid. After getting the confirmation, he ran back to the car with a slight smile on his face.

"You won't have to worry about him anymore, miss. He's over there dead as can be. Looks like you'll be safe."

Italy leaned her head back as the officer explained that they were going to have to hold her for questioning, and that an ambulance was on the way to check her out. Looking at Donovan's motionless body, she nodded and wondered what was to come next, now that this part was over.

"Is there anyone we can call to let them know you will be at the hospital?" the cop asked, tightening the blanket around her naked body.

Italy scratched her mother off the list without any hesitation. She and Tanya hadn't spoken much since Donovan was released, and the last thing she wanted to do was come back to her with drama. Jason was really the only person she wanted to be around at the time, and his face and charisma stuck out the most in her frantic time of need.

"Can you call my friend, Jason, for me? Please don't let

him know everything that just happened. I will do that myself. Just please tell him that I need him. Here is the number. His name is Jason Wright."

CHAPTER 12

The phone rang loudly, waking Jason from a deep sleep. He flung his arm in a panicked automatic response, knocking it off the receiver. Jason rolled over the side of the bed and hung his head between his legs. His eyes blinked uncontrollably for focus as the moonlight was his only line of sight in the dark room.

The answering machine clicked on.

"Leave a brief message, peace."

"I need to change that," he groaned to himself.

The clock read 5:00 a.m. He reached for his cigarettes as Bino's voice came over the machine.

"Jason, wake up, son. Pick up the phone, it's very important."

Jason blew the smoke out of his nostrils as he glanced at the phone. Bino's voice sounded urgent.

He picked up the phone and groaned, "What's up?"

Bino was snappier than ever before.

"We need to talk. Meet me at the spot."

Jason stood and walked to the doorway. He peeped in the living room and caught a glimpse of Italy's silhouette before walking back to the bed.

"Now?"

"No, give yourself a chance to wake up and *meet me at seven*."

His last words were sharp, causing more alarm than worry.

"What is this about?"

"I'll explain when I see you."

Jason hung up the phone and took another drag from his cigarette. He stretched out across the bed and flexed his muscles until the bones cracked. Silence filled the room and haunted his mind with pictures of the past. He thought of mornings he'd done this same thing, with Sheila snoring next to him.

His eyes darted from the clock to the ceiling as minutes crawled by. The phone rang again, making him jump in the solitude. He picked it up on the second ring, rolling his eyes.

"I'm up, Bee," he whispered into the receiver.

"That's good, man, because I need to come through."

"Sav?" he said, jumping to his feet. "Where are you?"

Silence came from the other end.

"Sav?" Jason yelled.

"Yeah, I'm here. Something don't seem right, Jay. I think they're on me."

Jason inhaled his cigarette and sat down.

"Look, go back to the house and I'll be there in a few hours. Are you on the street?"

"Yeah, I'm at a pay phone."

"Sav," Jason said, in his mildest voice possible. "What did I tell you? Stay in the house, blood. I asked you to listen to me. I can't help you if you don't listen."

Savion cut in.

"Jay, have you been watching TV?"

Jason exhaled. "You know I haven't."

"They have me on Oakland's Most right now!"

"Wanted?" Jason replied.

"What the fuck you think?"

"Shit!" Jason yelled.

"Go back to the house. Matter of fact, stay where you are.

I'm on my way right now. Don't call anyone and stay in the car."

"Hurry up, Jay."

"Calm down, and do what I told you. Paranoia will get you caught up. Stay calm."

Jason hung up the phone and put on a pair of sweats and dingy t-shirt.

Italy was sitting up on the sofa bed when he walked into the living room.

"Is everything all right?" she asked, turning on a light.

"Everything is fine. Get dressed. I have to drop you off at the Bart station."

"Now?" Italy asked. "I wanted to make you breakfast."

"Yes, *now*, Italy," Jason yelled.

Italy jumped at his outburst. She quickly got out of bed and put on her clothes. Still in pain from the beating she received just two days earlier, her face stung as she attempted to yawn.

"May I wash up, Jason?" she asked, holding her jaw.

Jason saw her hurt and lightened his mood.

"Yes, the towels are in the bathroom closet, and extra toothbrushes are under the sink. I really need you to hurry up, though. Some things just popped up."

The phone rang again. Jason snatched it on the first ring.

"Where are you at?" he said, already knowing it was Savion.

"I'm at Taco Bell in Union City across the street from Logan High School."

Jason hung up the phone and put the cigarette out. He put on a hooded sweatshirt and grabbed his keys.

"Come on Italy, no time for the pretty shit."

Italy rushed out of the bathroom and grabbed her things.

"Are you going to put on some shoes?" she said, glancing at his Nike flip-flops.

"Let's go!" he said, opening the door.

Jason sped out of his parking stall, turning the radio off when the music came blaring over the speakers.

"Jason, what's going on? Talk to me." Italy said, concern

stricken across her face.

Jason slowed the car down to the legal speed limit. The sun cracked its eyes over the sky and made a violet color through the clouds.

"One day, I'll tell you, if all goes right. Right now, I have too much on my mind."

Morning commuters began their day and clogged the streets in desperate traffic as they tried to get to work. Jason checked his watch over and over.

"Where are you staying at?" he said, approaching the 880 freeway entrance.

Italy studied the road as she thought about her temporary living situation.

"I got in touch with a friend last night, and she said it was good for me to come over and stay until things got back on track."

Jason glanced at her sulking face out of the corner of his eye.

"Where were you staying before?"

Italy swallowed the anger, she desperately wanted to scream out as the thought of El and Bianca watching Donovan try to kill her crossed her mind.

"With someone who will get theirs, as soon as I get things back on track."

Jason shook his head.

"You can do what you want, but some advice would be to let everything that has happened up until now, go. If you keep going backwards, you will never go forward in life. Just some advice for you to think about."

Italy thought about what he said before nodding her head. A tear came to her eye as she suddenly thought about her mother and wanted nothing more than to be next to her. Jason saw her tears and handed her a napkin from the center console.

"So what city are you staying in," he said pulling up to the San Leandro Bart station.

"Union city." Italy said, wiping her eyes.

"Where at?" Jason shouted fully alert.

"My friend stays right behind the high school in the apartments across the street from the Bart station."

"Good, I'll drop you off. I'm headed that way now." Jason said as he sped out of the parking lot.

The two of them rode in silence until reaching Hayward. Each thought about the other's circumstance as the traffic thickened, then thinned. Jason turned the radio on Wild 94.9 to tune into the T-man show, a local morning talk show on the bay area's second favorite radio station.

Italy turned the radio down as she stared Jason directly in the eye.

"So is there going to be a next time?" she said, leaning back in the seat.

Jason slowed the car to the flow of traffic.

"Yeah, maybe, I have to sort a lot of things out right now. I have way too much going on in my life. When I find some calm, I'll find you. Your situation doesn't make things easier. I'd push you away with my mood swings and refusal to accept anything but the best. That's all I'm used to, Italy. Sheila gave me her best, and I gave myself the best. A careless, sleeping in a different friend's house every week, insecure stripper is not the best for me. At least not right now. When I have time to know you, maybe then."

Italy turned from him and stared out of the window.

"Jason, why do you constantly talk to me like that? Are you trying to make me feel like shit? Does this stroke your ego and make you feel better by tearing me down?"

Traffic slowed to a stop. Jason reached for a cigarette, but looked at Italy and put it back in the pack. Exhaling, he ran his hand over his head. "Have you ever heard of destroy and rebuild? This is life, Italy. If things were sweet for you, I'd be sweet to you. But they're not. Would you truly respect things if they were given to you on a silver platter? No you wouldn't. No one would. I make you really look at how fucked up your situation is. Look at all the things you've had to endure. Instead of building off it, you dig your hole deeper. I can't pull you up. You have to first want to get up. The only way you'll want to get up is if you are forced to look at your life. Then the things you used to think must be destroyed and rebuilt with the right fundamentals to get you where you want to be in life."

Italy smacked her lips.

"Damn, you make me sound like a robot."

Jason shook his head slowly.

"One day it'll all make sense."

Italy stared at the now bright blue sky as they rode the rest of the way in silence.

Finally, Jason pulled in front of the Bart station.

Italy stared at the side of his face until he looked back at her.

"Your face looks old," she said. "Stress and those cigarettes are killing your shine. You need to quit one or the other."

Jason smiled.

"I'll think about that."

Italy leaned over and kissed his cheek.

"Can I continue to use your number, Jason?"

"Don't call me with any drama."

"I promise I won't. I respect you too much to do that."

Jason stroked her fingers and knuckles gently.

"Be safe, Italy. I have to go now."

Italy ran her fingers over his head before getting out of the car. "Destroy and rebuild, huh? We'll see, Jason."

Jason watched her walk off before speeding out of the parking lot.

CHAPTER 13

Savion was laid in the backseat as Jason approached the car. His arm was positioned under the passenger seat, gripping tightly to a small 380. Jason tapped on the window, startling him. Quickly catching a glimpse of the gun, he backed away from the window. Savion sat up slowly and looked around. Jason scanned the area for anyone suspicious before nodding his head to get out of the car. Savion quickly jumped out and got into Jason's car.

"Didn't I tell you to stay calm? Why the hell are you laying in the backseat with a gun?" asked Jason.

Savion let his seat down and tucked the gun underneath it.

"Put your seatbelt on," Jason said, driving down Alvarado Niles.

"Jay," Savion said. "You don't know what the fuck I'm feeling right now. You ain't on the run, nigga. Your face wasn't on a fucking TV show. How the fuck am I supposed to stay calm?"

Jason got on the freeway headed back to Oakland.

"What did the TV say?" he said, keeping an eye in the rearview mirror.

Savion lit a cigarette while massaging his left temple.

"They put it out there, man. The drugs, the murder, me

being an ex-con, you name it. Everything to make me seem crazy as fuck."

Jason's grip tightened around the steering wheel.

"See where your senseless thinking has gotten us? Do you know what? I'm not even going to go there with you. I'm done preaching. Do you still have all your money?"

"Yeah, it's in my duffle bag."

"Good! I'm going to drop you off at my spot. Stay your ass in the house, Sav. I have a run to make. I'll be back in a few."

"Where are you going?"

"I have to meet Bino. He called this morning, sounding fucked up."

"Let me go with you. I need to cop some weight."

"And sell it where, nigga? See, that's the shit I'm talking about. Should I just drop your dumb ass off at the police station? Damn! Think, Sav. Just fucking think for once in your life."

Savion smacked his lips and relaxed in his seat.

"I gotta get out of Cali now, Jay. This just ain't working."

Jason exhaled and nodded.

"I know, I know. We can bounce in a few days. Give me a minute to make a few things happen."

"Naw Jay, you're not coming with me. I'm not going to be the cause of you ending up in a fucked up situation."

"It's a little too late for that, don't you think?"

"It doesn't need to get any worse. I'ma go somewhere and lay low."

Jason pulled up in front of his apartment complex.

"We'll talk about it when I get back. Stay in the house."

"Aiight! Jay, why it smell like perfume in here? You had a bitch in here?"

"We'll talk later," Jason said, putting the car in drive.

"Bout time," Savion said, slamming the door and running up the stairs.

CHAPTER 14

"Have you eaten?" Bino said, adding sugar to his steaming black coffee.

Jason shook his head, tapping his fingers on the table.

"You already know there isn't much to offer, but put something on your stomach. Coffee and cigarettes isn't a healthy diet. You're losing weight."

"I know," Jason said, waving for the waiter.

Bino looked as if he'd aged ten years in two weeks. The waiter took Jason's order of steak and eggs, then hurried off to deal with the morning rush. Jason stirred his coffee as Bino sipped his. Silence fought between them as Bino stared into his cup while Jason paid direct attention to his every move.

"You're too jittery. I have never seen you like this. What is going on?"

Bino steadied his hand as he looked up at Jason.

"You know me too well. You listen too much."

Jason laughed as the waiter refilled their coffees.

"I only listen to what's beneficial. What's going on, Bee?"

Bino bit his bottom lip as he stared out the window. His eyes slowly moved back to Jason.

"I had to move Trish and the kids out of state."

His haunted eyes made Jason stop moving.

"For what?" he said, matching his stare.

Bino exhaled.

"I knew I could trust you. It's good to know one of my pupils doesn't bite his teacher."

Bino patted Jason's hands and leaned back in the booth.

"What happened, Bee? Stop beating around the bush." Jason whispered, leaning over the table.

Bino's smile faded.

"My home was raided two days ago. Early in the morning, I stepped out to get my paper and opened my door to police in my face with guns. My family was awakened to the same thing."

Jason bit the inside of his cheeks. Bino's eyes were distant as he thought in silence, recalling every moment of that morning.

"Who do you think is talking?"

"I don't know. It could be anyone. Someone I do business with could be getting watched. It could be anything, Jason. I'm being watched right now. I saw the same car follow me from the house to here. The only reason I continued here is because I know you live a clean life now."

Jason stiffened and let his eyes circle the room.

"They're sitting two seats up," Bino said, watching him.

Jason sipped his coffee calmly.

"I have an idea who gave them the information. The man was arrested two weeks ago with a large amount of weight and was released with charges that only carry eight months in the county jail. So we have a dilemma. It doesn't take a rocket scientist."

The waiter brought the food to the table. Jason put his plate to the side and continued sipping his coffee.

"Thank you," Bino said, grabbing his fork and knife.

"Eat, Jason! Stay calm. Your hand is shaking."

Jason put the cup down and stared at the food.

"I lost my appetite."

"Force it!" Bino said, shoving a fork full of eggs into his mouth.

Jason cut at the steak and forced a piece of it into his mouth and relaxed once he began chewing, then cut another piece.

"Feel better?" Bino asked, smiling.

Jason nodded his head.

"Why are you so calm?"

Bino wiped his mouth and took a sip of his orange juice.

"It was bound to happen one day. Like I always tell you, stay prepared for the worst. They didn't find anything on me or around me. All they can do is watch. But the question is, what are they actually watching? Nothing but a man going to work every day and having breakfast with a friend. So once they see they have nothing, the next move will be on him. I can guarantee he'll make the wrong one."

Jason washed the steak down with water.

"Be prepared, Jason, because you will now be followed also."

Jason sat the glass down slowly as he thought about Savion.

"That isn't good, Bee."

Bino looked up from his plate.

"Why not? You aren't doing anything, are you?"

"No, no! But…" Jason exhaled and leaned in close to him.

"Sav ended up on Oakland's Most Wanted list."

Bino stopped chewing and wiped his mouth again.

"Let me guess," he said, talking with his hands. "He came running to you?"

Jason shook his head.

"No! I found him. I had to, he's my brother and he's all I have left."

"Damn," Bino said, leaning his head against his palm. "Do you have him with you?"

Jason nodded.

Bino began cutting up his chicken fried steak.

"You have to get him to somewhere safe until all of this calms down. Do you still have some money?"

"Yeah, I'm still nice."

"Okay," Bino said, shoving a fork full of eggs into his mouth again. "I have a house in Clear Lake my uncle left to me when he passed. It's completely safe. There are no neighbors for miles. I want you to get him there as soon as possible. I don't agree with this, Jason, but I don't want to see you go down for aiding a fugitive. I understand completely. Most wanted, huh?"

Jason nodded.

Bino reached into his pocket and slid him the keys off his key ring. "Get him up there fast, Jason. He'll be safe until all of this blows over."

Jason took the keys from under his plate as Bino took another sip of his orange juice.

"So how are you going to get him there?"

"I'll think of something," Jason said. "What are you going to do in the meantime?"

Bino smiled.

"Continue working. Trish is coming home tonight. I'm not dealing with anyone until I get to the bottom of this. My lawyers are well paid, in the meantime. Finish your food. What else is going on in your life?"

Jason dug into his plate.

"Writing."

"About what? You're always writing about something."

"I'm trying to push a book. I have everything in my head, but every time I sit down to write, I go blank. When this is all over, I'm going to school for it."

"I think that'll be a bad move."

"Why is that?"

Bino pushed his plate away and leaned back in the booth.

"The best writers are natural. School only makes you focus on the rights and wrongs. The best writers never studied for it. They took their life experiences and things in their environment, and made art. I think you're a natural."

"Do you think so?"

"What do you want me to do, stroke your ego? I just said I do. You have to think it for yourself. As long as we live, people will be drawn to reality. The things that are real. Why? Because it is assurance that someone is going through the same things they are. It's an escape from their lives, but at the same time, a guide on how to get through and deal with certain situations. So my advice would be to draw from your life."

Jason swallowed the rest of his water and pushed his plate away. "Damn, I'm full. I really needed that."

"Jason, have you started dating again?"

Jason's smile faded as he rolled his eyes towards the window.

"Naw man, I'm not ready. Really, I don't want to. I'm cool the way I am. There's this one girl I keep running into, but she's not right."

"What's not right about her?"

Jason shrugged.

"She's a hype chick, Bee. Not my type. I try to lace her on things, but she doesn't listen. I'm not going to make somebody I don't know, with problems, *my problem*."

"You mean she's not Sheila?"

Jason didn't answer.

"Jason, Sheila was one of a kind. There is a reason she was taken so young. But imagine if neither one of you were taught the things you know now. I'm pretty sure this girl has it just as bad as the two of you did. You didn't listen to anything either, but I stayed on you until you got it right. There's a reason you keep bumping into her. Have you two had sex?"

Jason shook his head.

"Naw, she stayed over last night, but I didn't touch her. It just doesn't feel right. I know I can, though. That's just the last thing on my mind, especially with the things going on now."

"Don't worry about the things happening now," Bino said, looking over the check.

"This will all work itself out. Stay cool and calm at all times. Don't make any unnecessary moves. They could be your last. Are you ready to go?"

"Yeah, I need a smoke."

"You're really trying to kill yourself, huh? You really need to leave those things alone. They only add to the stress. Get Sav up to the house ASAP. Have it worked out before you get home. Here is the address."

"Ok, I'm going to get him out of there as soon as it gets dark."

"Good move," Bino said, standing up and stretching as Jason did the same while they walked to the cash register.

Jason glanced at the two white men wearing tourists' clothes, sitting in the booth directly across from the register. Jason caught one of their eyes and held it.

The man looked long and hard at Jason's face before turning away.

Bino paid for the food and turned around to face them. As he walked out of the restaurant, Jason didn't smile as he glanced back at them one last time.

Once inside their cars, Jason put up the peace sign to Bino and drove off.

Emeryville seemed to have more traffic than usual. Jason waited at a red light and let his thoughts run a million miles an hour.

"*How the hell am I going to get Sav to Clear Lake without me leaving too?*" he thought.

Checking his rearview mirror for any familiar cars, he took the address out of his pocket and looked it over, slapping it on his hand a few times before pulling off. Jason got onto the 880 freeway headed back to Oakland. He flipped through his CD case for something to soothe his mind. Carl Thomas was his final choice as he approached the 580/880 split.

CHAPTER 15

The sky was clear, and San Francisco seemed larger than life across the bridge. The sun sat on top of the Transamerica building, giving life to the city. Jason put his shades on as "Emotional" came over the speakers. His thumbs tapped the steering wheel as he maneuvered through the traffic. Slowing to a stop as Caltrans workers worked on one lane of the freeway, Jason continued checking his rearview mirror for any trailing cars.

Seeing nothing, his mind roamed back to the situation at hand. "Damn, Savion is like delivering a brick," he mumbled to himself.

Suddenly, his eyes got big as golf balls as the words left his mouth. Quickly he dug through his backpack for his cell phone and dialed the number in his head.

"Hello," a cranky voice said on the other end after the fifth ring.

Jason turned the music down.

"What's up, baby girl?" he said smoothly.

The voice on the other end woke up.

"Who is this? I know this ain't who I think it is?"

"Who else you know would call you this early in the morning? What's good, Fina?"

"Ahh, nothing, baby. Why haven't you called me? You

know I been worried about you."

"I had to get myself right."

"I understand, Jay. Sheila's passing fucked me up too. Angel has been asking where her godmother is. It hurt my heart to have to explain it. It made me think of you more. Are you back on your game now?"

"Yeah, I'm working my way back. How about you?"

"Money is slow as fuck, but I'm managing. I haven't caught any cases or anything."

"That's good, because I need you right now, Fina. I need you tonight. Are you up for it?"

"Damn Jay, why you had to fuck up the flow? That makes it look like you only called me to do something for you."

Jason pulled off the freeway at the Fruitvale exit.

"Now you know I don't mean it like that, but I'm being honest. I need your help."

"You know I'm here for you, Jason. What's up?"

Jason found a parking spot in the shopping center. He left the car running as he sat on the hood.

"Can you still hear me?"

"Yeah," Fina yelled back into the phone.

"I need you to take someone up to a house in Clear Lake for me." Jason said, a little excitedly.

"That's it? There's nothing with it?"

"Nope!"

"Yeah, I'll do that for you. Who is it?"

"Sav," Jason said, slowly.

The phone went silent.

"Fina, you there?" Jason asked.

"Yeah, I'm here. Jason I seen that nigga on TV the other night. He's way too hot."

"I know, but I have him tucked right now, but he can't stay out here. I can't take him because some other shit just went down, and I can't take the risk. I need someone I can depend on."

"Why can't he drive himself?"

"Fina, I want a trustful pair of eyes on him. By himself, he'll do something stupid. You know how he is."

"What makes you think he'll listen to me?"

"Because you're there on my behalf, and I'm the last person he wants to piss off. I just need you to get him there and that's it. Come on back when you do. I'll keep Angel with me. You will get four thousand for it."

"Four thousand, just for driving your brother to Clear Lake?"

"Yes!"

"Oh hell yeah. When do you need me? Right now?"

"Calm down, greedy. Call this number and let Sav know you're on your way to get him and that he needs to be ready. I'm going to call him as soon as I hang up."

"Okay, but I'ma leave Angel with my mom. No disrespect."

"None taken! Do what you need to do and I will call you back in an hour."

"Okay baby, let me go get this girl ready and I'll holler in a minute."

Jason hung up the phone and looked around at all the passing cars. Nothing looked familiar as he tried to calm himself and turn off the car. He lit another cigarette and started towards the Lucky grocery store as he continued looking over his shoulder, picking up the pace as he passed through a group of people moving a little too slowly. Sweat crept down his brow as he pulled out his cell phone and dialed the home number.

A white man of slender build matched his pace as he tried to keep up with him. Jason noticed the man's steps behind him and became more nervous. The man's beige trench coat blowing in the light breeze caused Jason to speed up.

The man caught up to him and put his hand on Jason's shoulder. By then, Jason had hung up his phone. He quickly stopped and looked to the sky as he swallowed and turned to face the man's piercing blue eyes. Jason was caught in his gaze as he focused on a spot right above the man's broad nose."Hi there! How are you doing today?" the man said.

Jason nodded at him, now looking at his dusty blonde hair.

"Are you missing anything?"

Jason's knees became weak as he stiffened and shook his head.

"I think you are," the man said, reaching in his pocket.

Jason felt like running. But what would he be running for?

The man handed Jason his wallet. "You dropped this over near your car. Man, do you walk fast! I had to almost sprint to catch up with you."

Jason eased up and smiled.

"Man, thank you. You don't find too much honesty these days. Let me give you something for it."

"No thank you. I looked in it, and saw that I had just passed you, so you deserve to have it back. A little advice, keep this in your front pocket."

The man patted Jason on the shoulder and walked off.

Jason leaned against the shopping carts and took a long breath from what was left in his lungs as he dialed his home number again.

Savion picked up the phone on the second ring.

"Jay is this you?" he hollered into the phone.

"Yeah," Jason said, rubbing his head.

Stay calm Jay, he said to himself. Savion sounded nervous.

"Someone just called here a minute ago and hung up. It was probably that chick you had over here."

"Did she call?"

"Naw, I was just saying."

Jason shook his head.

"No Savion it wasn't her, it was me. I had to hang up real quick. Listen Sav, Fina is on her way to pick you up. You are going to a house in Clear Lake."

"Clear Lake! What the fuck is up there?"

"It's one of Bino's safe houses. It is out of the way. Some shit hit the fan with him, and now the boys might be on me. Either way, I don't want to risk it, so I'm getting you out of here."

"Jay, I'm not trying to go to no Clear Lake, man."

"This is the best thing for you," Jason said, raising his voice.

"I'm not trying to hear that hardhead shit right now, Sav. You are hot as hell, and we need to get you out of here to cool you down. Now Fina is gonna call when she is ready. Get some clothes together and take whatever else you may need. Call me when you get on the freeway."

"Why can't you take me?"

"Because I know they'll be watching me. So before they case the house, I want you out of there."

"Aiight man. I don't feel it, but I'm going to listen to you."

"Thank you," Jason said. "Now get ready, okay?"

Jason hung up the phone and walked further into the store.

After getting a few things to snack on, Jason's cell phone rang as he pulled into traffic.

"We're leaving now, Jay," he heard Savion say.

Jason exhaled and smiled.

"All right, man. Stay safe and call me when you get there. Put Fina on the phone."

"What's up baby?" Fina said.

"Write down this address and call me every time you stop."

Fina recited the address as Savion wrote it down.

"Fina, put Sav back on the phone." Jason listened to the E-A-Ski CD playing in the background.

"What's up, Jay?" Sav said.

"I just want to tell you that I love you man, and I'll be up there as soon as I can."

Savion laughed.

"Aiight, you soft ass nigga, I love you too. One hun-ned!"

Jason hung up and turned the Carl Thomas CD up to full volum

CHAPTER 16

"No, Kamal, I don't want to come over."

"What, you don't love me anymore? Why you acting like you ain't my girl?"

"Because I'm not your girl, Kamal. I haven't been your girl in a long time."

"Ahh Italy, come on. You know you'll always be my little chicken head. Don't start frontin' now. I need some of that good head you got."

Italy paused with shock. It had only been one day since she was with Jason, and the last words he spoke seemed to ring in her ear nonstop as she listened to Kamal degrade her very being.

"What did you just say? I know you didn't call me what I think you did," she said, looking into the receiver.

Kamal laughed long and loud as Italy felt the tears form in her eyes.

"That was so romantic, Kamal. Why do you talk to me like that? I haven't done anything to you to deserve that. Anything you asked me to do, I did, and you call your so-called girl a chicken head? Yep, that's the most romantic shit I've ever heard."

Kamal started laughing again.

"I know you miss this dick. Let me come pick you up. I need to drop a load for real."

Italy hung up the phone before he could finish.

"Why do I keep calling that fool?" she asked herself.

"That's it. I don't have anything else to say to you, nigga. I'm through with you, Kamal," she yelled at the phone, although he was long gone.

The phone rang again before she could finish yelling. Italy looked at it coldly before flipping the phone open.

"What muthafucka? Leave me the hell alone," she screamed into the phone.

"Damn girl, calm the hell down. Who got you this upset?"

Italy exhaled at the sound of Tanya's voice.

"I thought you were Kamal's dog ass."

"Why do you keep giving that fool your number? You know he don't give a fuck about you, yet you keep subjecting yourself to his bullshit. You bring it all on yourself."

"Anyway," Italy sighed into the phone. "It's about time you called me. I was starting to think you didn't want to fuck with me."

"It's not that, girl. It's just that… I don't know. I been busy with this nursing school and trying to get my life together. I really don't have time for the bullshit and drama, and I'm not downing you, but you got a lot of drama on your plate."

Italy bit her bottom lip at Tanya's response.

"I'm trying, Tee. I really am. Things are hard. I don't have any help. The only good thing that has happened is Donovan getting in that car wreck. I don't wish death on anyone, but he deserved that shit. The nigga was trying to kill me."

Tanya was silent on the other end for a few moments. Finally, she broke the silence.

"Let me come pick you up. We'll talk about it then. It sounds like you need to go shopping with me and get your head right."

"Damn, this is a pretty night. I wish every night could be this clear," said Tanya. "This is why I love the summer."

Italy kept her eyes on the stars shining bright in the black sky. The August night brought on a light breeze as Tanya drove out of the parking lot of Southland Mall.

"I needed that little shopping spree. Paul has been getting on my last nerve. All he wants to do is fuck and smoke, fuck and smoke. He don't even do shit anymore but sit around the house."

"He isn't studying anymore?" Italy asked.

"Yeah, but how long does it take to do that? When he is gone, it's all night. He always says he's with his boys, but comes home smelling like pussy. I just tell him he's slipping, 'you smell like her.' He always says, 'we were at a strip club.' I say, 'you couldn't call to let me know?' Then it gets crazy, and all the 'I'm a grown ass man' shit comes out. I'ma shake his ass if he don't step it up."

"At least you got somebody," Italy whispered under her breath.

Tanya stopped at a red light and exhaled.

"Sometimes having nobody is better than having someone that's all wrong."

Italy watched the reflection of the car's rims and paint in the Bank of America window.

"Are all men wrong? I mean damn, I've been feeling like something is wrong with me. Even the ones that are right, don't want to deal with me. That's why I keep calling Kamal, just for the attention. He's everything I don't want in a man, but no other man cares. He doesn't care either, but I'd rather deal with one old dog than a few new ones."

Tanya giggled to herself.

"Why is it that we need them anyway? Last time I checked, I could do bad by myself. I need to shake Paul and focus on getting further. Get my priorities into perspective so the right one will recognize this queen."

"That sounds just like the shit Jason told me last week."

Tanya quickly jerked her head towards Italy.

"Jason Wright? You still talk to him? That name makes my blood boil every time I hear it. I don't care what anyone says, I know he had something to do with what happened. How is he just gon not know where his brother is after some shit like that happened?"

Italy twisted her lips.

"He didn't have anything to do with it. Jason's problem is he cares too much about the people he loves or likes."

"I seen that fool's brother on the news, too."

"Who, Jason?"

"No, Jason is too cool for that. His punk ass brother. He did some more stupid shit. I swear I'ma shoot his ass if I ever see him."

Italy's eyes popped out of her head.

"That's why he rushed me out of the house."

"What house?"

"I stayed over his house the other night when we saw each other."

Tanya shook her head slowly.

"Wait, where was Sheila? I know they didn't break up."

"Sheila died."

Tanya slammed on the breaks, jerking them both forward.

"What happened?"

Italy caught her breath and made sure no one was behind them.

"Girl, what the hell is wrong with you? You're lucky no one was behind us."

"My bad, but what happened?"

Italy turned back and settled in her seat.

"She died giving birth. The baby didn't make it either. Something was wrong with him when he was born."

"Damn that's fucked up. How was he holding up?"

"He's hurt, you can tell, but he's still mean ass Jason.

He's lighting up every time we see each other, but the cold part is, I don't even get mad when he grills me. It kind of feels good to have someone care for a change. Especially a man."

Tanya let a slight smile creep across her face.

"Did y'all fuck?"

Italy shook her head.

"Nope! I don't think he's tripping off all that. He tells me I'm beautiful and all that, but he never pursues me. All he does is listen and preach. I have his number, but I'm not going to call. There's nothing I can do for him. I'm not going to stop dancing anytime soon. That is the only way I'ma get paid right now, since I dropped out of school. I feel the same as you. I need to get me right before I think about a man."

Tanya stopped at a red light.

"Damn where is everybody at? I ain't never seen Industrial this empty.

"I don't know."

Italy's eyes got big when she looked at Tanya. Two men ran at the car. Before Italy could scream, one of the men busted the window open with the butt of his gun. The other did the same on Italy's side.

The man on the drivers' side opened the door and put the gun to Tanya's head.

"Get the fuck out of the car, bitch," he said, pulling Tanya by the hair.

Italy's screams finally escaped her breath as the other man pulled her to the concrete.

"You lucky I don't pop you, bitch," he said, getting into the passenger side.

Italy screamed louder, hoping someone would hear her. A few cars slowed, but continued on their way. Italy got off the ground and ran to the driver's side to help Tanya. The car jacker was having a hard time pulling Tanya out of the car. Italy ran to help, but was met with the barrel of his gun. He pulled the trigger, but the revolver clicked. Italy flinched before being hit with the butt of his gun.

Tanya was finally pulled out of the car. She crawled to Italy's side as she moaned, holding her head. Things started to blur as she blinked her eyes to focus. The sound of the tires screeching was all she heard as she tried to focus on the car. Tanya pulled her into her lap to make sure Italy was alive.

Italy's eyes finally opened. Her head pounded as they struggled to their feet. Tanya began cursing and screaming. She ran to a nearby phone booth and called the police as Italy staggered behind her. Italy listened as Tanya screamed into the phone.

She finally hung up and hugged Italy.

"Are you all right, girl?"

Italy nodded.

Tanya rubbed her stomach where she was kicked, and began cursing under her breath.

"See this is why I'm about to get a fucking gun. I'ma just start shooting these fools."

Italy tuned her out and sat on the curb.

A police car pulled up to them as Tanya paced the street, screaming. Italy explained everything that had happened while trying to calm Tanya down. After a description of the car was given and medical attention denied, the cops left them standing where they were.

Tanya called Paul, but got no answer.

Italy called her mother, but the phone was answered by a voice recorder, which stated that the phone was disconnected. Italy tried the number again, but received the same message.

"That don't make any sense. My momma smoke like a broke stove, but the phone ain't never been turned off. Billy always makes sure the bills are paid."

Tanya sat down and put her arm around Italy's shoulders as she began to cry.

"She probably wouldn't even care anyway," she sobbed.

Tanya squeezed her tighter. Italy wiped her eyes and started to laugh. "I knew that shit would happen. My momma has me so emotional lately, that I always just start crying now.

Oh well. I know who to call."

Italy got up and dialed Jason's number.

"Who're you calling?" Tanya said, standing beside her.

"Hi Jason," Italy said. "This is Italy. I need your help, and I don't have anyone else to call."

Tanya looked out into the street as Italy described the situation.

Finally, she hung up the phone and exhaled.

"He's on his way," she said, sitting back down on the curb.

CHAPTER 17

"Is he asleep? Was the ride all right?"

Jason asked Fina in rapid fire.

"Calm down, baby. You always ask too many questions. You know I would have called you if anything happened. It's only a three hour ride, Jay, damn."

Jason felt sweat start to form on his forehead as he questioned Fina.

"Now is it cool for me to come on back home?" said Fina. "I don't want to be away from Angel for too long."

Jason noticed the nervousness in her voice.

"What's up with you, Fina? You so spooked."

"Jay," Fina exhaled.

"To be real with you, I am. This is the one nigga that scares the shit out of me. He's reckless and he doesn't think. Plus, I don't tell on anybody, but if the Feds try and hold me as an accessory to helping him hide…" her voice trailed as she fell into deep thought.

"I'm not leaving my baby," she said, finally.

Jason breathed heavily as he took in her words. He glanced out at the sudden rain beating against his window. Fatigue rushed his body as he ran his hand over his now glistening head.

“Come on, Fina. I know it’s not your problem, but being scared does not do anything for us. Call me when you get back in town.”

Jason hung up the phone and sat down in his recliner. His eyes roamed around the room and rested on the picture of him and Sheila. “Sheila baby, this is not the way things are supposed to be. Damn, I miss you.”

A knock at the door broke him from his trance. He rose slowly from the recliner and took his time getting to the door as the knocking became louder. When Jason opened the door, two plain-clothes police officers stood before him. They seemed identical in looks as Jason observed their faces. He knew them as the FBI agents that were following Bino.

“Can I help you gentlemen?” Jason said, closing the gap between them and the door.

“Good afternoon Mr. Wright. I’m agent Fields, and this is my partner, Baker. Do you mind if we have a minute of your time?”

Jason smiled.

“You’ve already done that, so let’s skip the formalities and get right to it.”

The two agents seemed to smile at the same time. Jason couldn’t help but grin at the silliness.

“What can I do for the two of you?” Jason said, folding his arms across his chest.

“Do you mind if we come inside?” agent Baker said.

“Yes, actually, I do mind. I need the air, and I don’t allow strangers into my home, even the good protectors of the community.”

Agent Baker shifted his feet as Fields continued smiling.

“You’re real cocky, just like your buddy, Bino,” said Fields. “What’s your relation to him?”

“Private!” Jason said smoothly. “Meaning it’s our business. No disrespect, of course.”

“None taken, but we have reason to believe he’s involved

in some very heavy things, if you catch my drift. I'm pretty sure you can."

Jason made sure his eyes stayed glued to Fields'.

"I'm sorry, but that one sailed right over my head. Can you rephrase the question please? My comprehension skills are a little low. I think I have ADD."

After his statement, Jason smiled at the stern faces before him.

"You're a real smart ass, you know that? Smart asses always end up on my shit list," Baker said, pointing a finger in his face.

"Easy, Baker," Fields said, pulling his finger out of Jason's grinning face.

"Wow! Law enforcement still uses the good cop, bad cop, thing? I just knew you guys had a new tactic," said Jason, sarcastically.

"Look fellas, I'm going to level with you. Bino and I are friends. He saved my life when I was very young, and we still keep in touch because of it. Anything else is out of my knowledge."

"How did he save your life?" Fields asked.

"That again, is our business, sir."

Baker became flustered.

"What's with all the bullshit, Wright? We just came to ask a few questions."

"And I gave you a few answers," Jason cut in. His smile faded.

"Look, I have some things to do, if you don't mind. Is there anything else I can help you with?"

Fields clapped his hands together.

"No, that'll be all, Mr. Wright. If we have anything else, we'll be in touch. Oh, by the way, you haven't seen your brother as of late, have you?"

Jason shifted his feet without breaking his stare.

"No, we don't keep in touch. I haven't spoken with him in over five years. Why, what's the problem?"

Fields smiled a full wide grin, showing his coffee and tobacco stained teeth.

"No reason, no reason at all. Well, if you ever speak to him, tell him he needs to contact us to clear up his, um… *traffic tickets*. Give us a call if you see him, Jason."

Baker handed him a card before walking away.

Jason grunted and took the card between two fingers.

"I sure will," he said, in a pleasant tone.

"You two drive safe and continue the good work. We need more like you," he said smiling.

Fields stopped in front of him.

"I'm going to enjoy finding out your angle, because I know you know more than you are telling us. Have a good day, Mr. Wright."

Jason watched them get into their car and drive off.

CHAPTER 18

"I've found out who the one giving them the information is."

Jason looked up into Bino's face as he played with his daughter hours after the Feds visited his home.

"Go into the house with mommy," Bino said, patting her on the back.

Jason watched the little girl as she ran into the house. His mind suddenly flashed back to Sheila, pregnant, and the way her stomach poked out when she smiled. Jason stayed fixed in the direction of the house.

"Jason!" Bino snapped, bringing him out of his trance. Jason focused his eyes back on him.

"Are you okay?" Bino asked, looking into his face.

Jason nodded as Bino sat down in a chair.

"I just flashed back to Sheila that quickly," said Jason. "Who is it?"

Bino poured a shot of Hennessey into his cup.

"Why haven't you moved on?"

"Moved on from what?" Jason asked.

"Please don't act stupid now, Jason. You need to replace the past."

Jason sighed.

"I am," he lied. "You'll see. Just give me a minute. Who's doing the talking?"

Bino smiled as he leaned in next to him.

"I know you, Jason. Do you forget? I won't hound you now, but expect it when this is all over. Now, you don't know this man. He stays in Omaha."

"Nebraska?" Jason asked.

"Yes. Anyway, he was arrested a few weeks back with a couple of bricks, and amazingly did no time. He calls me last week and tells me he needs eight more as soon as possible. It doesn't take a genius to add these things up."

Jason nodded.

"So what now?"

Bino rose to his feet.

"We wait. That's all we can do and that's all we will do. The Feds are just fishing. They have nothing."

"They don't sound like they are going to be letting up anytime soon. That Fields guy really wanted to know about us."

"You told him the right thing, and that's good. Just keep your nose clean, and don't talk over the phone."

"They asked about Sav."

Bino stopped and looked at him.

"Jason, I really don't like this, but this is your call."

"Well, I have it set up for him to get out of the country, so let's just get that done."

"Make sure he doesn't leave that house." Bino said.

"Don't worry, he won't. I wanted to go up there, but I know they're watching."

"You're right, so keep it all on a pay phone out of your apartment. There's no telling what those fools will do, or how far they'll go. Some of those movies really tell the truth. You know all the bugs and things?"

"Bee, there's no telling how long this shit will last. From what I know, they'll stay on you more if they have nothing."

Bino shook his head.

"You may be right, but I'm going to let this all play out.

You just take care of yourself and stay out of the way. The last thing I need is for something to happen to you. I meant it when I said you're like a son to me."

Bino patted him on the shoulder and massaged the back of his neck. "I want you to get on top of whomever or whatever you're doing to get Savion out of here. There's only so long he will stay up there or in the house. With everything else going on, we don't need it."

Jason put his hands on his face and slowly let his fingers roam the creases.

"This shit is stressing me out, Bee. This isn't the way things are supposed to be going. I'm tired, man."

"When you get Savion out, I want you to take a vacation. I'm going to pay for it. Go somewhere and clear your head. Anywhere you want to go. Come back and finish your book."

Jason exhaled and pulled his keys out of his pocket.

"I have a few errands to run. I'll call you tomorrow."

Jason kissed Trisha and the kids before leaving the house. He put in San Quinn's *The Rock* CD and put it on "Done Deal." The speakers rattled as he turned the volume all the way up. The bass perked him up, making his shoulders bounce as he pressed harder on the gas pedal. He rapped along with Quinn, pointing his finger at everything he saw.

The muggy day made the bay look grey. The Hilltop area of Richmond looked livable, compared to what lay across the train tracks in North Richmond. Jason hurried up and got on the freeway, speeding towards Hayward. His eyes darted back and forth to his rearview mirror. He noticed a small Ford Escort trailing him as soon as he came out of Richmond. Jason's grip tightened around the steering wheel as he quickly switched lanes while the Escort did the same. Jason sped up and watched the speedometer rise to 90mph as he continued to switch lanes. The Escort stayed one car behind him as he approached the Hegenberger Exit in East Oakland.

Jason switched to the far right lane and slowed down as the escort pulled right behind him. Jason kept his pace as the exit approached. The music was turned up louder as the exit became closer. He smiled at Baker's wide frame, driving the car as Fields stayed focused on his car. Jason continued driving as if he wasn't going to take the exit until the last second. The Diamante swerved as he jerked the wheel towards the exit and stepped on the gas as a car sped up behind him.

The driver hit the brakes as Jason continued forward, watching the Escort continue down the freeway. He caught a glimpse of Fields watching him, while yelling to Baker.

He slowed at the stop light and sped down Hegenberger into a Denny's parking lot and parked in the back of the building before ducking into the restaurant. The restaurant was half-empty as he gathered his composure and took a seat in a booth facing the street. "Can I have a cup of coffee?" he said to the young Asian waitress as she walked by.

"I don't mean to stop you on your way to handle someone else, but that's all I want."

"No problem," the Asian woman said, smiling.

"Thank you." Jason focused on the passing cars, searching for the aqua colored Es.

The waitress came and poured his coffee quietly. Jason handed her a twenty and told her to keep the change. He watched the road. Finally, after ten minutes, Fields and Baker drove by the restaurant looking in all directions. Jason kept his eyes glued to the car as he sat, unnoticed. Once they were out of eyesight, he finished his coffee and cautiously left the scene.

CHAPTER 19

"This club is gonna be popping tonight. They're throwing a party for Chris Webber. It's his birthday or something."

Italy listened to her roommate, Jewel, as she stared at herself in the full-length mirror on the closet doors. Life had gone on, now that Donovan was gone and El and Bianca were behind her. Two weeks had passed since she'd last seen Jason, but even he was becoming a mere memory.

"You might mess around and knock something tonight, girl," Jewel said, applying her make up as her dark chubby frame jiggled when she laughed.

She pulled the straps of the skintight bodysuit over her shoulders and turned around to examine her butt in the mirror as Jewel continued talking. Italy tuned her out and thought about the catch she would get tonight. She ran her hand over her ample butt and slapped it twice; smiling at the fact that her body was becoming fuller.

Jewel lit a joint and sat on the bed, admiring her.

"Damn girl, I don't know how you do it, but you look good in everything. You gon catch hella flies tonight." Jewel passed her the joint as she sat on the bed.

"I don't need all those fools on me, just the right one. You know half of those idiots just look good, but don't have anything to go with it." The smoke filled the room as Italy lit another joint. She put her heels on and modeled for herself in the mirror again.

"We gotta hit the malls tomorrow and come up on some new gear. Jessica called today for a new coat. We're going to be busy boosting all this stuff."

"Yeah, I know. Junebug said he'd give me a 'G' for like ten fits with the shoes."

"What?" Italy said, shocked. "Where is Junebug getting all that money?"

"He has something with some videos going on. He went to LA a few months ago and came back caked up."

"Videos? What kind of videos?"

Jewel started giggling.

"It damn sure wasn't a movie-movie. That fool does the porno shit. Tisha told me he had a big ass dick with his ugly ass."

Italy stared at Jewel as she spoke.

"The broads get paid hella money, too. I heard it's like two or three Gs. I'm cool though. I got too much self-respect for that."

"Girl, you fuck these fools you'll never see again for free, so why not?"

"I'm cool. It's just not my style."

"Well I'ma get these fits for Bug and have a nice long talk with him. Come on Jewel, we can get papered up for real and come back stunting too. Do what we want instead of trying to help everybody else shine."

"Umm-umm Italy. I'm cool. AIDS runs too wild down there. I would think about something else if I was you. What about Jason?"

Italy stopped moving at the sound of his name.

"He's too smart, not that I'd try to work him. I feel something special for him, but Jay don't let girls like me get close to him. You gotta admit, Sheila was a boss bitch. She didn't flirt with cats or anything. She stayed fly and handled her business.

That's what Jason is used to. Those are some big shoes to fill. I can't get Jason's attention on that level until I'm correct, and all this bullshit is behind me. I'll have him eventually. But now, he just won't let me get close to him. He has some other issues going on. Anyway, I get depressed talking about Jason Wright, so let's change the subject. Besides, I'm about to catch me a ball player tonight."

CHAPTER 20

Club 17 was packed. Mercedes Benzes and high priced SUVs all on chrome wheels lined the streets and parking lots. Scantily clad women walked their most seductive walks, showing the smooth talking men their goods as they stunted in suits and other silky fabrics. Italy and Jewel walked a block from their car, catching catcalls along the way. Both were covered by leather trench coats, waiting for the right moment to unveil their masterpieces. Italy checked all the women out, suddenly becoming nervous at all the competition. The same complexioned women with thicker bodies were all over the place in packs.

Once inside, Italy took off her coat as she tried to look in the eyes of a few cute guys she had seen, for a reaction. The response was mild but still enough for her to feel relevant amongst the competition. As she made her way to the bar, a few men grabbed her arm to talk, but she shrugged them off, not ready to mingle and definitely not ready to deal with perpetrators and fake ballers.

Jewel wasted no time merging into the crowd, trying to get some attention. Flirting with a short, light-skinned man, her fake laugh was loud and nauseating.

Italy felt sets of eyes on her frame as she approached the

bar.

"Damn girl! You are working that. Come on over here and let me holla at you."

Italy smiled and brushed the gold-toothed man off. It was too dark to tell what he looked like, but she could see he was tall and skinny. Leaning into the bar, she ordered a Long Island Ice Tea as OutKast and Sleepy Brown's "I Can't Wait" thundered through the speakers.

As the night went on, Italy seemed to attract everyone that wasn't right for her. One by one, she dismissed them. Five drinks later, she spotted the VIP area and made her way over to the ropes. The smell of weed smoke floated from the booths as she looked on with excitement. The bouncer asked for her name and searched the list. Italy knew her name wasn't on the list, but felt she just might have a chance anyway.

"You ain't on here, ma. Can't let you in," the bouncer said, putting his hand up to stop her from looking in.

Italy tried her luck and began flirting, attempting to get a rise out of him. She brushed her breast against his huge chest and softly caressed his arms. The bouncer pushed her off as she became more aggressive.

"If you're doing all this to get close to me, cool, but I still can't let you in," he said, brushing her hand off him.

Italy stepped back and flipped him off, while making her way back to the bar with an attitude. She ordered another drink. Before she could pay, a dark hand reached over and closed her purse.

"Pretty women shouldn't have to pay for a simple drink," he said, handing the bartender a hundred dollar bill. He turned to walk away.

"Thank you!" Italy yelled. The man came back and leaned in close to her ear. "It's nothing. What's your name?" he said, breath smelling like a fresh mint leaf.

Italy became lost in the smell of his cologne. His muscular frame under a silk shirt brushed against her back and shoulders, exposing the rock hard muscle. She looked down and admired his peach colored gators and sharp creases in his cream-colored slacks. His skin was a smooth chocolate, setting a nice contrast to the cream and peach outfit he wore.

Italy liked everything she saw, down to his diamond pinky ring.

"Italy," she yelled into his ear, over the booming music. "What about you?"

"Maurice, everyone calls me Reese. What're you doing sitting over here looking as good as you are without dancing? And why do you have that ugly frown on your face?"

"They wouldn't let me in the VIP. That bouncer is a fucking jerk."

"They wouldn't let you in? With that outfit on? That's crazy."

Italy smiled at his tinted eyes.

"You like my outfit?"

Maurice took her hand and twirled her around, getting a glimpse of every curve.

"It says a lot," he said, caressing her arm.

Italy felt a tingle in her stomach.

"What does it say?"

Maurice smiled and licked his lips. He leaned in close to her ear again and breathed lightly, making Italy's heat rise.

"To me it says you're the baddest and sexiest *and* you're confident as hell. Your body is banging in that, sweetie."

Italy brushed a piece of hair from her face.

"Reese, what's up, boy?" A voice yelled over the microphone. Maurice put up a peace sign and continued his conversation.

"Somebody is famous, I see," said Italy.

"Naw, I'm just good with people. Me and the DJ go way back."

"Why did you hand the bartender a hundred?"

"Somebody's nosey, I see."

Italy giggled.

"No, just curious."

The bartender handed Maurice a bottle of Hennessy Privilege.

"So we can drink right," Maurice asked,

"You with me?"

Italy took his outstretched hand and followed him across the dance floor. People said hello and made themselves known to him all the way back to the VIP. Italy stopped and frowned at the bouncer as she made her way in.

The bouncer shook his head as he shook hands with Maurice. A group of beautiful girls looked on, trying to get his attention, hoping to be in Italy's shoes for the night.

The bouncer leaned in close to his ear and whispered.

"You know that bitch was just out here trying to do anything to get in?"

Maurice smiled as he looked at Italy.

"Is that right? You were just standing out here trying to do anything to get in?"

Italy frowned more as the bouncer smiled.

"That's not cute. Take that frown off your face, girl," said Maurice. "That doesn't look good on you at all. Can I get that beautiful chick I met at the bar again?"

Italy smiled as he smiled.

"That's better," he said grabbing her hand again to proceed.

"Stop hating," he said, slapping the bouncer on his chest.

Italy cut her eyes at him as they walked through the ropes. The weed smoke took her by surprise as she focused her eyes in the darkness. Stars of all walks sat in the booths with beautiful women caressing, laughing and trying to get in where they fit in.

"Is that E-40 over there?" she whispered to Maurice as they sat down at their table.

Two other men sat at the table with three other girls. The girls cut their eyes at her and made frowns at Maurice.

"Ty, Chris, this is Italy. She was having a little trouble getting in the door."

Ty and Chris nodded their heads at her.

Maurice introduced her to the girls to an ill-received response.

"Now, y'all gon act nice, or are we gonna have a problem?"

The girls rolled their eyes as Italy sipped her drink. Maurice leaned over and whispered in her ear.

"Don't even worry about these strippers. My attention is on you and that cat suit. Can you model for me one more time?"

Italy smiled, rose out of her seat seductively and turned around slowly. She twisted her hips, making sure to poke it out as her butt faced him.

"Damn," Chris and Ty said in unison.

Ty whispered in Maurice's ear as she sat back down.

"Look at her lips too blood. I know she give some stupid head."

Maurice laughed and nodded his head.

Italy smirked at the other girls as she took her seat. Chris and Ty left the table with the girls as Italy focused all of her attention on Maurice, zeroing in on his ring.

"Nice ring."

Maurice held his hand out to look.

"Yeah it is, huh? My wife got it for me a long time ago."

Italy almost choked when the words left his mouth.

"You're married?"

"Yep, happily too."

"Then why are you hollering at me?"

"Who said I was hollering at you? I just like what I see. It's okay to talk and look right?"

Italy looked away at the rest of the people in the room.

"Why does everyone know you?" she asked, turning back to face him.

"I play football," he said, matching her stare.

"I play for the Raiders."

Italy bit her bottom lip as San Quinn's "Hell Yea" blared over the speakers. Italy's mind switched to seductive mode as she grabbed his hand and led him to the dance floor. They danced for three songs, with Maurice feeling every part of her body. Italy felt as if her body was luring him to her and she flaunted it care free to everything else around.

"Can we go somewhere and talk?" she whispered in his ear.

Maurice smiled and led her to the door.

Italy waved at Jewel who was rubbing her booty into a chubby guy's groin. Jewel knew what the wave meant and nodded her head at the chubby guy.

Italy ran over to her and yelled in her ear, "He's a football player. I'll holla in the morning."

Italy got her coat and hooked her arm in with his as Maurice led the way to his Range Rover.

CHAPTER 21

Maurice let his seat down as Italy unzipped his pants and began kissing and licking up and down his manhood. Maurice laid back and felt himself stiffen as she put him into her mouth. His eyes rolled into his head as she slowly bobbed up and down, releasing a glob of spit onto his dick as he hardened all the way.

"Damn," Maurice yelled out as her lips tightened around his shaft.

Italy looked up at him and sucked harder as he held the back of her neck. She cupped his balls in her hands softly and sucked on them one by one.

Maurice moaned her name as she untied her top and let her breasts hang out. He pulled her closer to him and began kissing her neck and sucking and massaging her breasts. Italy moaned out as her nipples became erect. Maurice blew lightly on the wet spots he left, sending sensations through Italy's body as she pushed him back and began sucking him again. Maurice put both his hands on her head and locked his fingers in her hair. Italy sucked long and hard as he moaned, while Alicia Keys played on the radio.

"You ready to fuck me?" Italy whispered in his ear.

Maurice smiled and pushed her head back down to his protruding manhood. Italy looked at him with a question on her face as she began sucking furiously, this time using her hands to massage his chest.

Maurice felt his cum rising. His toes twisted in his shoes and his butt tightened as he suddenly exploded into her mouth. Italy quickly pulled back and began spitting the semen back out. Maurice laughed as she twisted her head from side to side, cursing him.

"What the fuck are you laughing at?"

"Don't act like you ain't tasted it before. It all tastes the same, baby."

Italy wiped her mouth.

"You should've told me. A girl likes to be ready for that."

Maurice glanced at her as he wiped himself off with a wet nap. Italy began kissing his neck. Maurice zipped his pants up and started the truck. "Put your top back on," he said. "We can get pulled over with those things out."

Italy tied her top again.

We must be going to a hotel, she thought. She actually felt somewhat confident in her oral skills and thought about all the things she would do to him once they got alone in a room. Maurice switched CDs and put on E-40's "Gasoline." Italy livened up and began bobbing in her seat.

She leaned over and began kissing his cheek and neck again.

"You don't know what I'm going to do to you tonight. I want to give you all of me."

Maurice smiled as he pulled in front of the club.

Italy pulled off him and looked around, confused.

"What're we doing back here?"

Maurice put the truck in park.

"I gotta get home. I have a long day tomorrow."

Italy rolled her neck and frowned.

"Oh hell naw! You aren't just going to shine me off like that. You think I just do that for everybody?"

Maurice rolled his eyes in her direction.

"Thank you," he said, smirking. "Give me your number,

Italy. Believe me, I want to kick it with you for real. You're hella pretty and cool. I ain't gone lie, either. Your head is crazy. I just want to do it right, next time. We'd be rushed and I want to take my time with you. Can you forgive me? I promise I'll make it up to you next time."

Italy's frown faded and was replaced with a grin.

"Well, I guess I can. Maurice you're just hella cool. You don't find that too much. You didn't try to stunt on me or shoot some bullshit. It seemed like you're real laid back and I want to be around you. I promise I won't come between you and wifey."

"That's cool. I'ma call you tomorrow when I'm done with my business.

"Well do you think you can drop me off at home?"

Maurice looked at the crowd of people emptying out of the club. "There's your friend right there ain't it?"

Italy saw Jewel walking quickly by herself to the car. Italy pressed the window down and yelled her name then turned back to Maurice.

"Call me," she said, kissing his cheek.

Maurice nodded as she got out of the truck and quickly drove off when she closed the door.

"Wait," Italy yelled after the truck.

Jewel walked over to her.

"What, you forget something, girl?"

Italy shook her head.

"Naw, let's go!" she said, as the thought of not giving him her number blew into the wind.

CHAPTER 22

"Yo' Champ, your boy is out here to see you."

"Who the hell is my boy, Seany?"

"That big head black boy."

"Jason?"

"Yeah man!"

"Hell, let him in."

Jason heard the latch to the heavy metal door slide to the side. Seany stood humongous in the darkness. His bulging stomach could be seen bouncing as he slammed and locked the door.

"What's up, young blood?" he said, wiping his face.

Jason nodded. "What's up with you?'

"Oh," Seany exhaled. "I can name 99 problems, but a bitch ain't one."

Jason grinned as Seany's whole body bounced as he laughed.

"Where's Champ?" Jason asked.

Jason felt a heavy hand grip his shoulder.

"It's about time you came to see your old uncle, boy. How long did you plan on hiding?"

Jason stood and embraced him tightly. Champ's huge frame seemed to swallow Jason. 6'5" of old hardened muscle;

Champ's golden frame was in contrast to the darkness in the room. Jason could see two old women sitting in the corner eye-ing every move he made. Weed smoke filled the air as they laughed at Jason's nervousness.

"You can come over here, youngin'. We ain't gone bite you unless you ask," one of them yelled.

"Y'all shut the hell up," Champ yelled. "My nephew is here. Matter of fact; take y'all old asses in the back. He don't need to see two ashy ass hookers. Get, now!"

The two women continued laughing as they left the room and Champ sat down.

"Sit down, boy!"

Jason looked into Champ's grinning face as he sat down.

"Damn, you're looking more and more like your daddy every time I see you. Why haven't you been by here to see me?"

Jason shrugged. "A lot has been going on."

"I can tell. You seem real calm, like you grew twenty years older over night."

"It was almost like I had to."

Champ lit a cigarette and took a light hit.

"Don't trip on anything. Things always work themselves out. How's that girlfriend of yours?"

Jason sat back and exhaled.

"She passed away."

Champ started coughing as he nearly choked on the smoke.

"You shitting me?"

Jason shook his head.

"She died giving birth to my baby. We had got out the game and everything."

"Damn, I'm sorry to hear that. How long ago was this?"

"Now you know I'm not going to answer that, because the first thing out of your mouth would be why I didn't call the Champer."

"That long, huh?"

Jason laughed as Champ forced a smile.

"I hate to hear that, Jay. I really do, but man you have to let me know these things. I promised your momma I'd look after you. How can I do that if you don't holler at me?"

"The last time I came through, Champ, you were in the pen again."

"Well, I had to do a little violation. They should really just leave a man alone after a certain age."

Jason giggled as he watched Seany serve coke out of a slot in the door.

"That's a-1 too, boy," he said through the door.

"Business is good, huh?" Jason asked, leaning back in the chair.

Champ took another drag of his cigarette.

"Business is business. It's up and fucking down. I still have to worry about the damn OPD, so it can stall at any time."

"Big dog! Big dog!" Jason heard over Champ's Nextel walkie-talkie. Champ pulled it off of his hip and frowned at the young kids' voice.

"What boy?" I'm busy!"

"The Elroys just came around the corner. Tell Seany…"

"Ok, let me know their status."

Champ closed the phone and pulled out a brown paper bag. He counted out a wad of money, stuffed it in the bag, and put it in a newspaper.

"Jay, I don't know why I pay these crackers when I still end up in the pen anyway. Seany, is that Lewis and Berg?"

Seany peeped out of a crack in the wall.

"Yep," he said, rubbing his stomach.

"Here, take this out to them and tell them to keep up the good fucking work," he said sarcastically.

Champ handed him the newspaper, unlocked the door and watched until he was back.

"They said your name hasn't come in anything lately," Seany said, nearly out of breath.

Champ nodded his head as he sat back down on the ragged sofa.

"So what else has been going on?"

Jason looked at the floor, biting his bottom lip.

"I knew that boy would end up in a fucked up situation," Champ said relighting his cigarette.

Jason glanced at him out of the corner of his eye.

"Savion? Thought I didn't know yet? Shit, that boy is hot as fish grease. My advice? You are already smart enough to know."

"That's my brother, Champ."

"And your dear brother will be the end of you if you don't think straight. You have too much going for yourself."

"I really don't have anything going on except trying to keep John Walsh off of his ass."

Champ shook his head as he stubbed his cigarette out in the ashtray. "Listen, trust an old man for a second. That boy got too much evil in him to sit still. He'll get caught eventually. He ain't going alive either."

Jason was silent.

Champ patted his leg.

"Look, just be careful is all I'm saying. Sometimes you have to put your emotions aside and do what's smart. Over half of the mistakes your daddy and me made in our day were over our emotions. He had my back and I had his, even if either of us were wrong. Even after his death, I still tripped for years. A lot of blood was shed over your daddy. It was Rochelle's choice to try and get y'all away from everything. She taught you right. I was shocked watching you grow up boy. You're smart. The way you do business is smart. There are a lot of pitfalls in life, Jay. Stay in place. Don't try and out run life."

Jason took a long breath as he thought about the words Champ was saying.

"Champ, I have to try and take care of Sav as much as I can. He won't listen to anyone but me."

"For how long? How long will he continue to do that? The boy is already jealous of you."

"What?"

"Don't start acting stupid, boy. You know what I'm talking about." Jason thought back to the words exchanged at the cemetery.

"Alright, look. I came to cop and talk about something else, to tell you the truth." Jason said changing the sticky subject.

"I know the Cuban boy must be hot, huh?"

"I don't know. I haven't talked to him in a minute," Jason lied.

"How much are you trying to spend?"

"I need two kicks."

"I can only let one go right now. It's going real tough right now."

Jason poked his lips out.

"Come on Champer, it's your boy."

"I know who it is, but this old man has to eat too."

"Ok, it's cool."

"It's pure too, Jay. So sell it that way." Champ said as he disappeared into the back room.

Jason sat back and stared at Seany as he sat with his mouth open, taking deep heavy breaths. He drifted off to sleep with his head on his chest; his grayish hair pulled back into a ponytail as sweat dripped off his chin.

Champ came back with the dope and tossed it to Jason.

"Snap back, boy," he said breaking Jason's trance before looking over at Seany.

"Seany, wake your fat ass up! Damn, I swear if I don't do nothing else in my life, I'ma get your fat ass in the gym."

Seany snapped awake, mumbling under his breath.

"Jay, look, do as I tell you, son. I don't want to see you in the pen or dead. Then my word wouldn't be shit, and sometimes that's all a man has. So please, at least let me have that."

Jason nodded his head as he handed Champ the money out of his leather pouch. Champ put up his hands.

"No, you keep that. Seriously, just keep your promise. That will be payment enough for me."

"Champ," Jason exhaled. "Take this money, man."

"See, I knew you couldn't do it. You can't keep a promise can you?" Champ said rubbing his chin.

"Yes I can, but…"

"No buts, just do it. Keep your money."

Jason smiled and put the money back in the pouch.

"Promise me you'll come by more often. Matter of fact, my birthday is in a few weeks. Come and take me to dinner or a strip club or something. Ok?"

Jason stood up and gave him a hug.

"You got that, old dude. I'll be here."

"I ain't too old where I can't whip your ass, Jay. Don't make me do that. Get on out of here, now. I have to get back to work."

Jason put the dope in his waistline and pulled his shirt over it. Champ watched him, smiling.

"You're just like your daddy, boy. You got a stash spot in that car, right?"

"Yeah, I'm going to call you in a week. Oh, before I forget. I got someone I want to connect you with. He's a youngster out of Hayward, real sharp dude. He did a favor for me and I need to put him on for it."

"What does he have going on?"

"Tyrell Avenue! The whole thing is his."

"How the fuck is that? Last I heard your boy Gooney had that spot."

Jason popped a piece of gum into his mouth as he stared at Champ.

"Oh, I see," Champ said, waving his finger. "What did the boy do wrong?"

Jason nodded his head as he checked his watch. Champ laughed at the resemblance to Jason's father.

"Damn, you're just like your daddy, boy. Ok, I don't want to know. Whatever he did, it had to be serious, because that was your boy. Do you believe in the new youngin'?"

Jason nodded his head.

Champ looked him over as he thought about the

prospects.

"Ok, I will give the boy a try. What's his name?"

"Malikie. Trust me, Unc, he's a real soldier. He got a real go hard type of crew too."

"Why me and not the Cuban boy?" Champ asked.

Jason shook his head as he headed for the door.

"Something ain't right with him. I don't know what it is, but he's not being himself. I don't want to put the youngster on with something unstable. You are a lot of things, but I still trust you with my life, and I know you are dependable."

Champ smiled at Jason's compliment.

"Ok, call me when you are ready for that transaction. If I sense any foul play in him, I'm going to kill him on the spot, Jay.

"Ok." Jason said blowing a bubble in his gum.

"I'm going to call you next week so we can go out."

"You better," Champ said as Jason walked out the door.

Jason glanced up and down the street as he approached his car. He got in the car and hit the brake pedal three times, and the gas pedal five times before a slot in the center console popped open. Jason put the kilo in the slot and started the car as it closed, checking all mirrors before driving off.

Carlton Brown

CHAPTER 23

Everything seemed quiet as Savion walked along a dirt trail through what seemed like an endless amount of trees covering hills, leading into a small town. Beams of sunlight pushed through the Redwoods as Savion thought about the week he had spent up there gathering his thoughts and honestly wanting a life better for himself and the many kids he had fathered.

Clear Lake was more of a vacation getaway type of place. The locals were old and peaceful people, trying to enjoy the rest of their years without any problems. Savion took in the crisp fresh air as he stuck his hands in his pockets. He laughed to himself. The fact that this was the first time he hadn't had to have his gun on him in a long time seemed amusing. Kicking at a few rocks, he stretched his arms out as he approached the town. He looked around as he headed down the dirt trail, everything seemed normal. A few people watched him, but that was normal and to be expected.

"I bet I'm the first black person they seen in a minute," he said to himself.

Continuing through the small town, he passed a McDonalds and Taco Bell as he headed to a small Safeway to get a few groceries.

This is living, Savion thought as he pushed a basket into the store. Loving the fact that he hadn't had to look over his shoulder, he smiled ear to ear as he began putting condiments in the basket. Catching a few stares, he didn't worry a bit about who or why they were watching; all he felt was freedom and for the first time, alive.

"Excuse me, can you tell me where the cookies are?" he asked a courtesy clerk sweeping the floor.

"Lane three," the skinny white kid said, looking out through the store's front window.

Savion ignored what he was looking at and continued down the lane. Suddenly, a feeling of worry came over him as if he was back in Oakland. Savion stopped what he was doing and looked in all directions. No one seemed to be watching him, but yet, he still couldn't shake the feeling. He proceeded to pick up a few more things down the lane. Pushing the basket to the front of the lane, Savion stared out through the storefront window. Suddenly, his heart froze and sank to the bottom of his stomach as the basket continued rolling in front of him.

Quickly, he stood to the side and tried to get a better look out the window. Police cars and federal agent's vehicles scattered the area with their lights on. Five got ready to enter the store as the others held their positions. Savion crept backwards to the back of the store and hid between aisles as he thought about his next move. Getting out of the front door was impossible, but every store had a back door.

Savion crept to the back, being sure to look over his shoulder and all around him. He pushed open the receiving door and peeked his head out to see if there were any more cops in the back. Seeing nothing, he stepped out and silently let the door close behind him.

"What the fuck is going on?" he said to himself. "Somebody had to tell. That bitch, Fina. I knew she wasn't to be trusted."

Savion ducked fast behind a tree as a cop car drove through the receiving area. Looking up behind him, nothing but hills of trees waited with all their concealment. With no other way out, Savion ran as fast as he could up the small hill and into what could be considered woods. No one noticed him as he continued to run high enough so that he could look over the whole parking lot of the store. Law enforcement cars were everywhere. It seemed as if they had brought out the National Guard for one man. Without a doubt in his mind, he knew someone had told. Knowing he had to get out of the area and back to the bay, Savion continued walking until he came upon a small house sitting deep in the woods.

Savion crept by the bathroom window and peeked in. Seeing nothing, he proceeded to the back of the house where a 4x4 Ford F-150 sat dusty and dirty, but still drivable. Quickly, he ran to the truck and carefully tested the door. Slowly, it opened as he peeked from the side of the truck into the woods in front of him. Making sure to be as quiet as possible, Savion slid in the truck and immediately began searching for keys, or anything that would possibly start the truck. In the center console, he found a loaded 38 magnum with a set of extra bullets. He tucked the gun in his jacket pocket while continuing to turn the truck inside out.

After five minutes of frantically looking everywhere, Savion gave up and started to get out of the truck. Suddenly, someone stepped out of the house, stretching their arms as they began to stagger over to the truck. Savion quickly climbed into the backseat and tossed a blanket over him.

The driver, an old white man who could be considered humongous in his younger years, began whistling as he started the truck. Never paying any attention to the papers scattered over the seat, the man continued whistling as he drove through the woods until he reached the main road.

Savion peeked from under the blanket at the long straggly hair that the man let flow freely, and the thick bifocals he watched the road with. Savion held the gun in his hand in case he had to use it faster than expected. Knowing that he could pop up, take the truck and dump the old man, he continued to ride in silence, seeing how far he would be going.

"What the hell is going on up here?" the man said to himself as he passed Bino's place.

Savion moved very slowly as he rose up to see what the man was talking about. Police cars and federal vehicles combed the area in search of him. He recognized no one as the man continued to roll on, still whistling. Savion slid back down into the seat as the man drove another mile down the road.

Finally, the man came to a stop and rolled his window down.

"Good mornin' sheriff, what you boys got going on today?"

A deputy sheriff stood at the window looking into the truck.

"You haven't seen anything strange going on around here, have you, Harvey?"

Harvey shook his head as he spit a wad of tobacco into the street. "Nothing unusual, except all these damn police cars running around. Who you all looking for?"

The sheriff backed away from the truck.

"Some boy wanted in the Bay area for a couple murders. Somebody dropped a tip, saying he was up here. He's black, so he shouldn't be that hard to find. If you see anything, you call and let us know before you do anything."

"Will do, sheriff. You all have a good day," Harvey said as he drove off.

Savion laid in the backseat thanking God as he loosened his grip on the 38.

What the fuck am I going to do now? He thought.

Harvey continued to drive for miles through the woods, without a thought in the world about the danger lying in his backseat. Savion felt the need to kill him and hurry up back to the Bay area.

Without warning, Savion sat up and stuck the .38 into Harvey's neck. Harvey jumped in his seat, making the truck swerve as he lost control from the shock. Savion was tossed back for a second, but regained his composure and put the gun to his neck again.

"Be cool man, nobody needs to get hurt here."

Harvey looked at him through the rearview mirror.

"What do you want from me man? You can have whatever you want, just don't kill me."

Savion tossed the thought around in his head for a second. Knowing that Harvey would race to the sheriff's office in no time, he decided to kill him.

"Pull this muthafucka over, old man. I ain't gone do nothing to you."

Harvey continued to look at him through the mirror.

"You're the fella the sheriff is looking for, aren't you?"

Savion slapped him in the back of the head with the gun.

"Don't ask me any muthafucking questions," Savion said.

His hatred for the white race began to pour out.

Harvey pulled the truck over on the side of the road. Savion looked around for any signs of life as he held the gun tight to his neck.

"Shooting me won't get you nothing, young man. Please, why don't you let an old man go on back to his home to finish his days living in peace?"

Savion put the gun in his neck harder.

"You know what, old man? This is your lucky day. Get the fuck out of the truck."

Harvey complied with what was asked of him and stepped out quickly as Savion climbed over the seat. Harvey held his arms in the air as Savion shut the door and screeched off in his truck. Harvey watched as Savion suddenly stopped and put the truck in reverse backing up until he was in front of Harvey again.

"I changed my mind. You won't do nothing but tell, and I don't need the police knowing this truck."

Without another word, Savion pointed the 38 at him and let off one single shot, slamming into Harvey's right breast. Savion watched as he dropped before screeching off again.

CHAPTER 24

"Damn Italy, you're looking hella good. What've you been up to?"

"Nothing, just trying to make a dollar or two. Is the size right on the coat?"

"Yeah, it fits cool. How do I look?"

"You look tight, baby. Very clean." Italy stood in her living room as June Bug came out of the bathroom in the clothes she boosted for him. Ever since parting ways from El, she had been trying to scrape up a dollar or two by doing whatever she could to pay the bills.

"It fits you just right. You are going to have a lot of chicks on you in that. I hear you got a cold little stable going."

June Bug's pockmarked face spread as he smiled, showing off a row of diamonds covering his teeth. Italy tried to keep her eyes off his crooked left eye. June Bug was one of the neighborhood hustlers who had been trying to get with Italy for years, until he moved to Los Angeles and started a small pimping business running hoes from the Bay to New York.

"Your braids are tight too. Mmmm, mmmm, if you were my man, I'd be hella happy." Italy said, stroking his ego.

"We might be able to arrange something." June Bug said

as he modeled the coat in the mirror.

"Naw, not right now. I'm trying to get paid."

"Well why don't you just roll with me? You know I been feeling you for a minute now."

"Independent Bug! You heard the song."

June Bug laughed as he took another look in the mirror.

"Yeah, this'll work. How much I owe you?"

Italy stood next to him in the mirror. "It's on the house."

June Bug made a quizzical look. "For what?"

"I need something else from you."

"What?"

"I need you to hook me up in the porn biz."

June Bug started to laugh lightly. "Are you serious?"

Italy stood in front of him and looked him directly in the eye.

"I'm dead serious. Jewel told me you get down."

"Yeah I do, but that ain't you, girl."

"How you know what me is? I'm a hustler, nigga. I ain't got no time to sit around worrying about catching some nigga or getting some time for stealing these damn clothes. Bug, I don't even know you, nigga. If you'd take your mind off fuckin' me, you'd see the same thing. Now can you hook me up?"

Bug exhaled as he turned his focus back to the mirror.

"You know I gotta sample the product to make sure you know what you're doing?"

Italy rolled her eyes as she folded her arms over her chest.

"Damn Bug, are you that desperate to hit this? Come on, nigga. Think about the dough. Tripping off all this won't do nothing but have you frustrated."

"Damn, Italy don't put all those extras on yourself. That porn shit is a business for straight lazy ass toss-ups that can't do nothing else but fuck. So by you sweating me to get in the shit, it just lets me know your status so miss me with that bullshit you're pumping about yourself. Because we both know if I pulled out $500 right now and told you to suck my dick, you'd do it."

"Nigga please! You got me way fucked up."

"I do? What the fuck you think they gone tell you when you get down there? Can you please take your clothes off and nicely give him oral sex? Bitch please! You're gonna be every bitch and hoe in the book, before, during, and after the sex. So we might as well form some chemistry now before we get there. The shit is about sexual energy. That's what people buy it for. If you're a boring fuck, you won't make any money because no one is gonna want to hire you. So what do you want to do?"

Italy sat on the couch and ran her fingers through her hair. She slowly started to unbutton the buttons on her blouse. June Bug watched her through the mirror as she became fully naked. June Bug turned around and appraised her body.

"You're beautiful. Just like I always thought you'd look."

Italy rolled her eyes.

"Let's do what we do so you can get the hell out of here."

June Bug continued smiling.

"Put your clothes on, bitch. The scene ain't even right, Italy. I need you to want me. You gotta want the person you work with so the scene turns out right. You want to be explosive."

"And I'm ready, so come on."

"Naw, not now! In due time. I'ma take you with me to my next flick. We're gonna build you a buzz first, before you do a scene. I'ma manage you and make sure you get top dollar."

"Hell naw, Bug. You're not going to pimp me."

"Ain't nobody talking about pimping nobody. I'm making sure you don't get fucked over. This business is dirty as hell. Messing with me is the safest thing you could do."

Italy put her panties and blouse back on, and sat on the couch. Bug sat beside her.

"Look, I wouldn't feel right knowing I brought you into something and you got the shit end of the stick. This game is dog-eat-dog, and money over a bitch is the main issue. Be happy somebody is actually giving a fuck."

"How much does it pay, Bug?" Italy said in a whisper.

"Five hundred to a thousand a scene. I want to make it to where you get the top dollar."

"And how much would your cut be?"

June Bug stood up and stretched out his back.

"About $40 off every hundred. That ain't too bad, right?"

Italy shook her head as she grinned. "You're crazy. So you won't let me in unless I get on your team?"

"Basically! I don't see what the problem is. You get in this thing blind if you want to. You'll get your ass ran right back to Oakland. Plus, I got all the plugs for the magazines and strip clubs. I'm seeing the big picture, baby. You are thinking little dough. I'm thinking grown man shit. Grown people money. Think small, you'll get small, you dig?"

"How did you get this entire hook up anyway? How did you get in?"

June Bug smiled, unzipped his pants, and pulled his dick out.

"Any more questions?"

Italy's eyes became light bulbs.

"Got damn, Bug, you're packing for real!"

Italy held it in her hand and stroked it a few times. Her breath became faint as he hardened and became fully erect.

"Damn!" she exhaled. "I want you to fuck me now!"

Italy pulled her panties off and lay back on the couch with her legs parted. June Bug put his manhood back into his pants.

"See, that's the kind of energy I want. See how bad you wanted me? The director would've loved that shit. Now these next flicks I'ma take you with me and tell the director I want to fuck you. He'll pay you like $800 or $1,000.00. You can keep that. But you have to have this same energy when I take you down there."

"Don't worry about that. You pull that snake out at any time, and I'm with it."

"I'ma fuck the shit out of you too. I been wanting you for

a while."

Italy smiled as he complimented her features.

"When are we going, Bug?"

"It should be in a few weeks. So try to keep it tight."

"It'll be good." She said, putting her clothes back on.

June Bug opened the door to leave. "It better be. As much as I jocked you, it better be worth the wait. I'll holler in a minute. I got a contract for you to sign, too."

CHAPTER 25

"Italy… this is your mother. Can you please give me a call when you get this message? I really need to talk to you… I… I love you baby."

Italy sat on her bed and replayed the message over and over. Jewel was busying herself getting ready for work. Italy watched as she ran back and forth. Jewel rambled on as Italy stared at her. The words were not computing, as her mother's voice played over and over in her head. Jewel put on her high heels and continued talking.

"What do you think she wants?" Italy spoke.

Jewel stopped and sat on the bed.

"Who?" she said, buttoning her blouse.

Italy got up and walked to the window.

"My mother," she exhaled.

Jewel looked around the room in silence. She fought for the right words to say, knowing this was a touchy subject.

"Maybe she just wants to see you. It has been a minute now."

Italy glanced around the room. "Look at this, Jewel, look at how we're living. Don't get me wrong, I love it because this is the most stable I've been in a while, and I thank you for that. But this isn't supposed to be our life right now. We're supposed to be at home with our mommas going to college, not stealing clothes and stripping and all this other nonsense."

The tears poured from Italy's eyes as she fought to control them. She wrapped her arms around her chest as she sat on the bed and began rocking.

Jewel put her arm over her friend's shoulder, trying to console her.

"You just don't know the half, Jewel. My momma hasn't given a flying fuck about me in I don't know how long. It would take forever to tell you the story and all the things that she's done to me."

Jewel held her and listened.

"The one thing that hurts the most," she choked between sobs, "Is that she put a man over me. Her own child, she put her own child out on the street over a man. Now she tells me she loves me?"

"Maybe she wants to make things right," Jewel said. "I'm not trying to make excuses for her, but things happen, Italy. Their lives became way harder once they had us, especially with husbands running off and leaving them."

Italy shook her head and stood up.

"I can't accept that," she said, drying her eyes. "All I've ever wanted was for my mother to love me and help guide me through this maze. Everything I've learned I've had to learn on my own. That hurts. Learning to be a woman on my own? Oakland is a cold city. A girl can lose it all here. I'm about to do some damn pornos just to survive. I want to go to fashion school so bad, but I don't have the funds. I know about investments and everything, but I don't have the funds. Every nigga I bump into that I think is digging me turns out to be a fucking jerk. This isn't life, Jewel. Do you know how many times I've thought about just killing myself and getting it over with? I couldn't do it, though. I don't have the guts to."

Jewel stood up next to her.

"Italy, you're stronger than that. You're one of the

strongest people I know. I look at you sometimes and wish I had your strength. I don't know too many people willing to go out on a limb the way you do. You're a survivor, and sometimes experience is the best education. You have to go through it to become a master at it. You understand? Stay strong, sometimes we have to be our own rocks to stand up straight.

"You don't need that porn shit. Tell June Bug to go and fuck himself. We'll survive. That shit won't do nothing but make you more depressed. Look at Misha, she used to be a boss, now all she does is let niggas fuck her in vans all up and down the street and pop ex. If that's how she wants to live her life, more power to her. The same goes for you, but I know and you know, you're way smarter than that. Money doesn't bring anything but more problems. It's cool, don't get me wrong, but carry yourself with a level of dignity, and it'll come. You feel me?"

Italy nodded her head.

"Where do I start, Jewel? I see the vision but how do I get it started?"

Jewel grabbed her purse.

"First off, call Bug and tell him you're cool. Second, find out how much financial aid you can secure for school. We'll talk some more when I get off work. Call your mother, Italy. God forgives and so can we."

Jewel blew her a kiss as she walked out of the apartment.

Italy sat in silence. She picked up the phone and stared at the numbers. She could hear the dial tone thumping through her ears. Slowly, she dialed the numbers and waited for her mother's voice.

"Hello," a dry and cracked voice said on the other end.

Italy was silent for a few seconds. Beth repeated herself. "Hello."

"Hi Mom, it's me," Italy said, barely audible.

CHAPTER 26

"So what's the mystery behind Mister Wright? I've been thinking about that one question since we last spoke, man."

Jason shrugged his shoulders at Christian.

"No mystery. What you see is what you get!

Christian smiled.

"One day, Jason, you're going to let me in on you. You know women don't give up until they get what they want."

"I don't want you to give up."

"Really now? That leaves a challenge for me then, huh?"

"If you want to call it that."

Christian smacked her lips with ice cream on her mouth. They sat at Lords Ice cream shop in San Leandro. Jason admired the way the sun shined on her face.

"You look intense," she said, scooping another spoonful of her strawberry ice cream.

"That's one thing I'm learning about you."

"What's that?" he asked, swallowing his milkshake.

"You show your emotions on your face. I can kind-of-tell what you're thinking when you're thinking it."

"Really?"

"Really!"

"Then what would you say I was thinking now?"

Christian wiped her mouth and sat back in the booth.

"Kiss me!"

Jason laughed. "Gong," he said, imitating hitting a snare drum with his hands.

Christian reached across the table and hit his shoulder lightly. They both smiled and stared into her each other's eyes as Jason grabbed her hands and massaged them in his "Actually, I was thinking about how beautiful you are," he said. "You're easy to talk to."

Christian blushed.

"Then why don't you talk to me? You only tell me so much, Jason."

"Am I the only one? I think I've expressed myself a lot." Jason said.

Christian raised an eyebrow.

"Every time I ask you a question, if it's a good one, you'll answer. If it's one you don't want to answer, you change the subject."

Jason continued massaging her hands. He kneaded them slowly as he examined her nails, wanting to kiss her fingertips and feel her lips close to him.

"What do you have to say about that?" Christian pressed.

"Some things are best left unsaid, until the right time. Don't worry, I'm not a rapist or anything like that. I'm just a very personal person."

"Jason, I want to be a part of that person. I've been thinking about you almost every day for the last month. All I know about you is that you're deep, you're a writer, and where you want to go in life. I know you were my ex-boyfriend's best friend and partner, but I'm into you, Jay. Not love. Please don't confuse it. Just really into you. I don't mess with dating. I haven't done this in a long time, because there are just too many games and bullshit for me. But I saw something special in you the moment we met."

Jason held her hands tighter.

"I feel the same about you, but why rush things? I respect your morals and self-respect. That's hard to find in women these days. Believe me, it'll all make sense, soon," he said, smiling as he kissed her fingertips.

Her pout melted into a smile. "You're too cute. I don't know why I let you slide like that on everything. Come here, sexy."

Christian cupped his face in her hands and kissed him slowly. Jason continued poking his lips and kissing the air when she released. Christian laughed as she pulled her Gucci Bag over her shoulders.

"I gotta get back to work, Jason. Walk me back to my car."

Jason held his arm out for her and headed towards their cars, arm in arm. His phone chirped as they walked across the parking lot. "Hello?"

"Jay, it's me. Where are you at?" Savion was out of breath as he talked.

"Whoa, whoa, Sav, where are you?"

"I'm in the town."

"Why?"

"It got hot. I went to the fuckin' store and saw cops all over the fuckin' place. I dropped everything and cut. Somebody ratted. I bet it was that bitch, Fina."

Christian looked at him with worry in her eyes.

"What's wrong?" she mouthed.

Jason put his hand up and continued talking.

"Where are you now, Sav?"

"In the town, *fool*."

"Where, smart ass?" Jason's voice became angry.

"On 98th. I'm at a safe place. Come get me, Jay. I'm paranoid, blood."

"Stay where you are. I'm in San Leandro, but I'm leaving right now. Don't go anywhere, okay."

"All right."

"Sav, I mean it! Are you thumped up?"

"Yeah."

"Don't talk to anyone and stay on guard. I'm on my way."

Jason hung up the phone and started walking to his car.

Christian followed behind him. "Jason, did you just forget I was here?"

"I'm sorry," he said, continuing to walk. "I got an emergency I have to deal with. I'll call you later on, okay?"

"Jason, what's going on? Let me help."

"You can't help on this one," he said, opening his door.

Rushing, he stopped and came back to face her.

"I'll explain tonight, trust me. Okay?"

"I do. I really do. Call me on my cell as soon as you're done."

Jason kissed her and jumped in his car.

Christian watched him speed out of the parking lot.

CHAPTER 27

Jason turned his music off as he got off the freeway in the 98th block of East Oakland. Sirens could be heard in the near distance, making butterflies grow thorns in Jason's stomach. He turned onto East $14^{th,}$ and was faced with a roadblock. OPD had the intersection blocked off as they lined the street.

"Damn Savion," Jason whispered. A helicopter flew overhead with its search light beaming through the night.

Jason observed as people got out of their cars to watch the scene. He turned his car off and got out to get a better look. A brown Cherokee was crashed into the side of a McDonald's as an ambulance rushed the scene. Jason hurried behind the long line of onlookers. The police were beating Savion as they handcuffed him. Everyone stood in awe. Jason broke through the line and rushed towards them, but was grabbed and tossed to the ground. The knee in his chest took his breath away as he struggled to get up.

The big country fed white cop wouldn't let him up.

"What do you think you're doing, boy?"

Jason fought for air.

"That's… that's my brother."

The cop eased up and stood over him. He extended his arm and pulled Jason up.

"I advise you to stay right here and not proceed to the scene."

The cops backed away so the medics could lift Savion onto a gurney and rush him to the truck.

"Can I ride in the truck with him?"

"Out of the question. Your brother isn't a victim. He's the suspect. He just shot a cop and one other person that we know of. You won't be able to see him anytime soon."

"What rank are you?"

"Does it matter?"

"It's a question."

"I'm a Lieutenant."

"Why did you stand by and let those officers beat my brother like that?"

The cop let out a hysterical laugh. "Are you serious, son? Your brother just possibly killed a cop. You all would've killed him had we not caught him. Isn't that the way it goes? Ya know, black on black crime?"

Jason saw Savion's bloody body being lifted into an ambulance. The ambulance with the wounded cop had already sped away. Jason backed away as the Lieutenant watched the scene. He got in his car and drove off before he was noticed. He sped through the back streets until he reached Highland Hospital. Cops swarmed the area as news crews had already crowded.

Jason parked on the street and rushed to the emergency area. He fought to get through all the uniforms and people crowding the area to see what the commotion was. Two guards stood at the doorway. Jason was stopped as he tried to get through.

"Sorry son, we can't let you through here," said one of the guards.

"That's my brother that was just taken in there!"

"The shooter?" the other cop asked.

Jason didn't answer.

The first cop talked into a radio, informing a sergeant of his presence. "Stay right here," he said after he was done.

"Look, I just want to know the condition of my brother, nothing else."

"I can tell you that now," a voice, low and gruff said behind him.

Jason turned around to face the short, chubby, sergeant. His double chin jiggled when he spoke. Jason frowned down at him. The sergeant's pants looked as if they were going to burst.

"He's been shot four times. It looks like he isn't going to make it."

"Four times?" Jason asked.

"Yep! The stupid fucker shot one of our best. In the throat, *at that*. He's lucky we want him to live right now. You have a real idiot for a brother. Did you know he was a wanted fugitive? Of course you knew. The Feds are on their way here, now."

Jason bit his lip and looked at the floor.

"What is your name, son?"

Jason looked from the floor into his fat face.

"Jason. Jason Wright."

"How did you know he was here?"

"I was driving by and saw the commotion like everyone else. Is this necessary?"

"Very," he responded quickly.

"Where were you at about 5:30 p.m. today?"

"In San Leandro with a friend."

"What's your friend's name?"

Jason thought about Christian. He knew he didn't want to drag her into his madness.

"Yolanda. Yolanda Stevens."

"How can I get in touch with this Miss Stevens?"

"If I'm not being arrested for anything, that's none of your business."

The sergeant smiled, "You're a smart ass, huh? Must run in the family. Stupidity, that is. That's what has your damn brother lying on a stretcher like a slab of meat. I hope he survives. I want to personally kick his ass every day I can. He's going to wish he was dead after we're through with him. Now get your ass out of here. If ya come back, I'll arrest ya and beat your ass myself. One brother is just like all the others in my eyes."

Jason's fists balled as his mind began to see nothing but red. He bit his cheeks until he felt and tasted blood. The other cops stood looking at him, waiting for his response.

The fat sergeant smirked at him.

"Go ahead and do it. I dare you. It'd be my pleasure to book your ass." Jason un-balled his fists and walked past him. Other cops tried to get in his way, but he avoided them, only brushing shoulders as he walked quickly to the sliding doors of the exit.

"Jason!" a voice yelled after him.

He stopped to see Tanya running to catch up with him. She wore her blue scrubs clutching a clipboard in her hands.

"Jason, do you remember me?"

Jason nodded.

"You're Italy's friend, Tanya, right?"

Tanya nodded.

"I saw what they did to you in there. If you need a witness to sue, I'm here. But that isn't why I caught up with you. Savion isn't going to make it. He got shot in his lung, eye, heart and thigh. The thigh shot pierced a main artery and he's lost a lot of blood."

Jason balled his fists and banged it against the wall.

"How long?"

Tanya shrugged.

"I don't know. Depends on how strong he is. They aren't going to let me get too close, because I'm just an intern, but I took the ambulance report. Jason, I'm not gonna front and say I'm not at all happy. Savion deserved what he got. That's the way he lived. Especially after what he did to me and Italy. But I am sorry for you, and that this had to happen this way."

Jason turned and looked down at her face. He couldn't be mad at her. Savion did put her life in danger. Patting her on the shoulders, Jason thanked her before walking out.

Tanya watched him leave through the doors.

The night was crisp and the winds started to blow lightly. Jason reached in his pocket to retrieve his cigarettes. Savion was right down the hall, and he couldn't get ten feet in front of him. He lit his Newport and inhaled deeply, hands visibly shaking as he pulled the cigarette from his lips. The cell phone rang as he blew the smoke out. The ID screen flashed Christian's cell phone number. Jason inhaled the smoke again and turned the phone off, stuffing it in his pocket as he began walking to the car.

"Mr. Wright! Mr. Wright!"

Jason was tired of being called tonight. He wanted to just jump in his car and drive as far away as possible.

"What?" he said, turning around.

Agents Fields and Baker walked quickly towards him.

"May we have a minute of your time?"

Jason unlocked his door.

"Look, I really don't have time to deal with you two right now. My brother was just shot up."

"We know," Agent Fields said, doing all the talking as usual.

"Tragic. It really is. I wish we would've caught up with him at Clear Lake before this could happen."

Jason looked at him in surprise. "Clear Lake?"

Baker smiled and spoke up.

"Yeah, Clear Lake. Of course you didn't know right?"

"No, I didn't," Jason said.

"Right," Fields said, stepping towards him.

"You're good, Jason. Especially the way you left us on the freeway. Anyway, we're sorry for the tragic scene."

"Thank you," Jason said, getting into his car.

"One more thing, Mr. Wright. We really do wish we could have gotten to Savion before all of this. Our tip told us to arrive at the house early, so that we would not be detected. He said there weren't too many ways for him to get away if we surprised him."

Jason looked at him with a stone blank expression. Baker

tapped the roof of the car.

"Tell Bino we said hello," he said, before walking into the hospital.

Jason sat in his car in silence, the shock still sinking in. The cigarette burning his thumb snapped him back to reality as he threw the butt out of the window and drove off.

CHAPTER 28

"AIDS! We haven't talked in months, then you call me to tell me you have AIDS. How am I supposed to act, Ma? You're damn right I'm tripping!"

Beth sat on her dingy couch scratching her matted grey afro. She shakily flipped a cigarette in her mouth and lit it as she stared at Italy's raging face. Italy paced the dimly lit apartment where she grew up. She stopped and looked at a picture of her and Beth when they both were much younger.

"What do you want me to say, Italy?" asked Beth. "We all gotta go someday. My day has just arrived. That's all."

Her voice trailed off into a whisper as she inhaled her cigarette.

"You don't see me too worried, do you?" she said, flicking the ashes in an ashtray.

Italy turned on her heels. Beth saw the fire burning in Italy's light face as she turned red.

"Maybe that's the problem. You never care about anything. Not even yourself. How could you care about me? You know what, Ma? Mother, *my momma*, I'm through caring. I'm through shedding tears over you. Wanting nothing but your love when you love that damn shit-that… that damn crack-more than your own blood, your own daughter. Why Momma? Tell me. We're gonna get this out in the open now. I want to know why you always do this."

Beth rose to her feet and wrapped her arms around Italy. Tears streamed down both of their faces. Beth sat them down on the couch and stubbed her cigarette out as the silence engulfed the space between them. Italy sat back and wiped her tears away. Beth let them flow as she looked at her daughter.

"You're so cute, Italy. Look at my baby."

Beth tugged at Italy's Gucci jeans and top.

"Italy, look baby… there's really nothing much I can say. We both know I haven't been the best mother to you. I can tell you that I love you dearly."

A smile formed on Italy's face. She stood and looked at her mother's thin frame. *She is still beautiful*, Italy thought. Her smile disappeared when she glanced around the apartment.

"Why, Momma?" she asked, after an extended silence.

"Why what, Italy?"

Italy paced to the window.

"Why did you treat me like that all those years? Do you honestly think it's easy for me to just sit here and be all happy? As much as I've loved you, I've hated you as well."

Beth flipped another cigarette into her mouth. Italy snatched it and broke it in half before she could light it.

"Child, have you lost your mind?"

"It's a nasty habit that I can't stand. Now answer the question."

Beth smirked as she put her lighter back on the table. Italy came and sat back on the couch next to her as Beth looked deep into her eyes.

"My child, I owe you everything. I've been wrong for so long. It's easy to blame it on the narcotic, but that would be too easy, even though that played a big part. The other part would have to be your daddy walking out on me and you. That had to hurt the most. They go hand-in-hand, because one caused the other.

"But really, I can't be too mad at him because I was weak for letting that shit take me over. Anyway, when I was pregnant with you, that was like the most incredible feeling. Me and your daddy were inseparable. He couldn't wait to be a father. I just couldn't wait to get you out. You had me huge. Anyway, things started getting bad for us. Oakland was changing. Your daddy lost his job. I was too big to work, so your daddy started drinking real heavy and snorting a lot of cocaine. I knew he was running around with different women. We'd argue, but I never chased him. I didn't want to risk having a miscarriage. You were the most precious thing in the world to me.

"Anyway, your day finally came and your daddy was just out of it. I had to drive myself to the hospital and everything. He was off getting drunk and high somewhere, talking about how happy he was about being a father. So I went through labor and everything by myself. When you came out, I held you in my arms and kissed you so many times, but I knew your daddy was gonna be on some other level. You were so light. I knew the first thing that was gonna pop in his head was, '*that baby's not mine.*' Now for the record, I never cheated on your daddy. Never! I believed in my heart that he was mine and more than enough man for me.

"Anyway, he saw you and flipped out. I pleaded with him that I never cheated. He didn't want to hear it. He kicked my ass real good, and left with some woman he was fucking. I put you in my arms many of nights and chased him through Oakland. I even shot at that fool a few times. My whole life revolved around him. Your Grandma is light-skinned, just like you. That's where you get it from, my momma. Anyway, after so many years, I gave up. He never showed again.

"I started smoking and it hit me bad. You were growing real fast. I loved you, but the more I smoked, the more I started to hate you. I never got over your daddy walking out on me and I sorta started to blame you, like in some crazy way, it was all your fault. So the prettier you got, the meaner I got. That narcotic didn't help any. Then, I met Billy, he came with money and that's something I had none of, and he had plenty. I never loved him or wanted him, but he took care of us. He knew what was going on, but he never said anything. The times he did, I was so high that I would damn near kill him. So he stopped arguing all together.

"The one thing that hurt the most when I found out that I'm going to die soon was that I've been treating you like shit all these years. I put everyone and everything over you. That hurt the hell out of me, so I can imagine how you feel. There are no excuses, Italy. I certainly have none. I'm not going to cry over spilled milk. What's happened has happened, and there's no changing that. What we can change is our relationship. I want us to become closer. I don't know how long I have. I have full-blown AIDS, and no money to keep me breathing. White folks got a cure for it, but only for the rich. This is something else created to kill off our people."

Italy smiled at her mother's militant remarks.

Beth scratched her head.

"The first thing I want you to do is take me to a beauty shop. I looked in the mirror the other day and jumped at my own reflection. Malikie had me in a hotel room for so long, I started to feel locked up, but I understand what he was doing. He is going to go down in history one day."

The two of them laughed.

"How did this happen, Momma?"

Beth exhaled.

"Like I said, I didn't love Billy, so I was having sex with different guys."

"Unprotected?"

"No, well yeah, sometimes. Most of the time, I left it up to the man to put one on and if he didn't, well he just didn't. The doctor said I've had this for a long time and never even really knew it. Most of the time, I was so high I never paid any attention to any symptoms. I was drunk out of my mind and fucked with the wrong bastard. Everybody knows he got the sauce too. You have seen his ass before. Well that's who I think gave it to me, but to be honest, with it being full-blown, there's no telling where it came from. I can't believe I was so reckless, but it happened. I'm so thankful I had Malikie there to help me out, or else I would be in prison right now, trying to find you. How did he get a hold of you?

"I bumped into his friend, Whip, at Southland Mall."

"Oh ok. Well, Billy left me. He found out and left everything. Told me to go to hell and just left. All the money in the account is gone. I don't blame him. The one thing he asked me to do was just stay faithful, and he'd take care of everything else. So, I just have been sitting around here trying to piece everything together. The first thing I did was stop smoking that narcotic. The second is you. I can only say I'm sorry baby, and I hope you forgive me."

Italy patted her mother's thigh. They sat in silence for some time. Italy stared at her from the corner of her eyes.

"I forgive you, Momma. I do. It's hard as hell though. You don't know half of the things I've been going through. It's been pure hell. I blamed you for a lot of it. I chalked it all up to survival, which it was. I had to survive and I'm proud of myself for not getting killed or addicted to any drugs, but it's been hell. There were a lot of things I had to swallow. Some things I couldn't do anything about. Momma, I've stripped, sold my body for money, and had sex with dudes just to keep a roof over my head for the night. I got raped, Momma. Yeah. A fool raped me."

Italy felt the tears form in her eyes again as she continued.

"Billy tried to have sex with me. Tried to blackmail me into it, and you sided with him. We would've survived Momma, together! Together, we could've done it. I know how to get money and you do too. Even if it took us to get some jobs. We have to now, right?"

Beth nodded as she dried her eyes. "Italy, I don't know how long I have to live. I want you to come back home and stay with me. I don't want to die alone, and I don't want to die with things not being right between us. I don't want anything else to happen to you. I don't know if I'm healthy enough to get a job, but I got something else I can do."

"What's that?"

Beth stood up and walked over to the kitchen. She returned with two shot glasses and a bottle of whiskey.

"I was thinking," she said, pouring them both a shot. "I could invest the rest of the little money I have into some cocaine or weed, and survive like that. I don't do none of it anymore. That stuff is part of the reason I'm in the position I'm in now. So, I'm not worried about that. I know a lot of people who do both and as long as I serve good shit, clientele comes. Drink your shot, baby."

Beth downed her glass, smacked her lips and poured another.

Italy looked at her glass. She picked it up and sipped it slowly. The Jack Daniels tasted nasty to her and she sat the glass back on the table.

Beth laughed.

"You have to slam it, baby," Beth said, downing another shot.

Italy picked up the glass. She looked at her mother pouring another shot. This was the closest she'd felt to her in a long time. Sorrow for her mother crept in. The pain was visible in Beth's face as she smiled at her.

Italy massaged her mother's neck slowly.

"I guess I have no choice but to forgive you and be here, huh?

Beth clanged their glasses together in toast.

"The choice is yours. I can't force you to do anything, and I won't."

Italy threw the whiskey down her throat and frowned from the burn. She leaned over and kissed her mother's cheek.

"I'm not going anywhere. We will be all right while you're here."

CHAPTER 29

Jason floored his Mitsubishi across the Bay Bridge. Floetry's "Now You're Gone" played in his deck. He glanced at the cigarette ashes as they started to overflow in the ashtray. Heat began to rise around his collar as he hit the gas pedal harder, letting the window down slightly as the CD ended. It had been weeks since he last talked to Christian. After Savion's death, he went into his normal state of being closed off and tuned the rest of the world out. It took all he had to get out of his apartment and make the necessary arrangements to have Savion buried next to the rest of his family.

The funeral was attended only by him, and a minister from his mother's church. This minister had also done the other funerals.

"I've never seen nothing like it, Jason. Your predicament is unfortunate son, but we're here and the church is with you when you're ready to return. You all have always been in our prayers."

Jason tuned the reverend out and stared at Savion's face. He flashed back to the way Savion held him as they watched his father dead on the ground. The urgency in Savion's voice the last time they talked. The last words the two federal agents had said to him. They later enraged him as he approached San Francisco. He slowed his car down as he exited onto the Embarcadero, pulled into a Shell gas station and turned the car off.

The cool air felt good across his warm body as he took his button-up off and sat with the door open. He rubbed his hands over his head and stared at his cell phone. Christian had left a million worried messages on his phone. They turned angry and then finally stopped all together. He sat and listened to every one of them. The last one had him in San Francisco at 11p.m. in the now freezing cold. He put on his leather coat and dialed her number.

Becoming nervous as he looked in every direction, Jason almost hung up when he heard a male voice pick up the phone.

"Hello."

Silence was the response until the man repeated himself.

"Uhmm, I'm sorry. May I please speak to Christian?"

"Yeah, may I ask who's speaking?"

"Jason. Tell her it's Jason."

"Ohhh, you're Jason. Man, you're in a lot of trouble with my sister. You really pissed her off, not calling back. Do you know how many nights I had to hear that shit? I'm glad you called, bruh."

Jason half smiled at the fact that he was talking to her brother and not her new acquaintance.

"My name is Keith. She should be back from the store in about half an hour. Want to try back then?"

"Yeah, that's cool. Tell her I'm in Frisco and I wanted to see her."

"Do you know where she lives?"

"Yeah."

"Well, just come on through. I'll let you in. Y'all need to talk."

"I'll be there in about 10 minutes."

"I'll be waiting."

Jason hung his phone up and lit another cigarette before starting his car.

His thumbs twirled as he listened to Keith ramble on about school. Nothing had changed in Christian's apartment. As he looked around, he noticed a picture of the two of them on a glass shelf, and picked the picture up and stared at their smiles.

"Where did y'all go that day?" Keith asked.

Jason sat the frame back in its place. "Santa Cruz. That was our third date."

Keith stubbed out the joint he was smoking and blew the smoke out of his nostrils slowly.

"Jason, I'ma tell you, man, my sister really digs you."

He lifted his 6'5" frame off the couch and stretched his body.

Bones popped in his legs and shoulders. Jason noticed how big he was. His chest stuck out like the front of a Mack Truck and his legs were like tree trunks. Jason felt small next to him, thinking Keith had to make it to the NFL after college.

Keith continued,

"She doesn't really deal with men too much. She's too damn smart for the bullshit we do. Her last boyfriend was a jerk. She hasn't had a relationship since. I thought she was gay or something. Then you came along."

Jason smirked as he thought about Gooney. Goon was indeed a jerk, but he was also his friend and Jason hated that it had to end the way it did.

Keith poured himself a half glass full of orange juice and added Kettle One vodka to the other half.

"From what she's told me, you're kind of the same way! She said she's been fighting to get through your guards. I can see what she means. I'm just letting you know that Christian is cool."

Jason nodded his head.

"Thank you."

"No doubt," Keith said, as the keys to the front door jingled.

Christian came in with Keith's girlfriend, laughing. Jason's insides warmed at her laughter. Keith stood up and grabbed his girlfriend's chubby hand as Christian's laughter stopped when she saw Jason. He rose to his feet as Keith and his girlfriend walked back out of the apartment.

Jason heard her whisper his name as the apartment door shut. Silence invaded the room. Christian stared at him as she walked past him into the kitchen.

"Sit down," she finally said, once in the kitchen.

Jason did as she asked, as she stood at the entrance and folded her arms over her chest.

Jason smirked at her innocence.

"Is that the angry pose?"

"Do you see me laughing?" Christian responded quickly.

Jason exhaled and tapped his fingers on the arm of the love seat.

"Was it a bad idea coming here?"

Christian sucked her teeth.

"No. If nothing else, you owe me an explanation for all the worry. All the nights I sat up worrying about you, only talking to your damn machine. So, no, it's not a bad idea. Do you want something to drink?"

Jason rose to his feet and walked in front of her. Her breath became heavy as he took her hands in his. He stared at her until he put his arms around her waist and pulled her into him, hugging her tight. Christian wrapped her arms around his neck. Her hands ran over his head as they became consumed with each other. Jason pulled back and kissed her bottom lip softly as she felt tears forming in her eyes.

"I thought you were dead!"

"I felt like it."

"Why didn't you at least let me know you were breathing?"

"I kind of tune everyone out without warning when something bad happens."

"What happened?"

Jason ran his hands through her hair and kissed her top lip.

"Everything is fine. It's nothing to concern yourself with."

Christian began shaking her head. "No, no, no! That's not gonna work this time, Jason. You duck and dodge me for weeks, then show up in the middle of the night and expect me to just let it go with, 'it's nothing to concern myself with?' No Jason, before I even begin to forgive you, you need to let me know what the hell is going on!"

CHAPTER 30

Jason let his eyes roam around the room until they landed on the picture of the two of them. He looked back into her face and thumbed her tears away.

"You know what, Jason?" she said, taking a step backwards. "I don't even know you. I don't know why I'm tripping off you. You touched me, Jason. Do you understand? I've never met a man like you, and I latched on. But I latched on to someone I have to guess about. I don't like guessing about people. I like to know what and whom I'm dealing with. You're here in my home. I've only seen the outside of yours. I worried about you. You don't even call back to soothe my thoughts and nerves, yet, you're here and all I can think about is who the hell are you, and where have you been? You kiss me, and I let you because I feel a deep connection between us. I felt it the moment I saw you with Goon all those years back. Yet, you act like I don't matter, like I'm just for your convenience. Talk to me, Jason! You owe me that. If you walk out of here tonight, I want to know you, even if I never see you again."

Jason took her hands in his and led her to the loveseat. He sat her down and took off her coat, mouth suddenly becoming dry as he started to explain himself.

"I think I'll take that drink now," he said, rubbing his hands together.

Christian got up and poured him some of the vodka and orange juice.

"Bring the bottle. This is gonna be a long one." He said as he stared out of the window into the cold San Francisco night.

Christian handed him his drink and sat the bottle on her coffee table. She sat back in her seat and crossed her legs as Jason paced the floor, sipping his drink. He stopped and stared into her intense eyes.

"Did you hear about the police shooting in Oakland about the same, or last time we talked?"

Christian nodded.

"If I'm not mistaken, it happened that night when you left me at the ice cream spot."

Jason nodded as he sipped his drink.

Christian's eyes became light bulbs. "Jason, did you shoot the cop?"

Jason sat his drink down. "No. No, Christian I didn't. They got the guy who did it."

"Oh yeah," she said, calming down. "Well what has that got to do with you?"

Jason sat next to her on the loveseat. "That guy was my brother. That was my brother, Savion."

Jason poured another drink as Christian stared at him.

"Your brother? Okay."

Jason sat back on the couch.

"He got killed! He was shot by the police and died in the hospital that night. I saw them when they beat him and handcuffed him while he was shot. I tried to find out what his status was, but they wouldn't let me five feet in front of him. Plus, they dogged me on a whole other level. A friend told me he wouldn't make it."

"Why was he shooting at the police?"

"Because he was on the run from his picture showing up on the most wanted list for Oakland some time ago, for a handful of murders. So, he came to me and I had him out of sight in a cool place. Somebody snitched on him and they raided the town, but he saw them first and was able to make it back to Oakland. But Savion was a very hardheaded individual. When he called me, I told him to sit still, but he's always been a paranoid person."

"What were the murders about?"

Jason exhaled.

"Trying to compete with me. That's what it all boils down to. Instead of working together, we turned into two brothers or one brother competing against the next. He felt like I thought I was better than him because of the life I had. The woman I had, everything. I tried to force my way of life on him instead of understanding his way."

"The woman was Sheila?"

Jason looked at her out of the corner of his eye. He took a sip of his drink and swallowed hard, then smiled as he thought about Sheila.

"You already know," he said.

"We were each other's first loves. We came up and raised each other. She was my world after my mother passed. It's indescribable, the kind of woman she was. Completely loyal and devoted to me. A quick thinker and she listened to what I told her. She was beautiful. I loved her with every inch of my being because she understood me. I don't get into relationships, because no woman could match her in my eyes, and no woman could understand me like she did. She worked as hard as I did towards our future. I miss her, but life goes on, right?"

Christian ran her palms over his arm slowly.

"How did she die? I heard she had passed, but I didn't know how."

Jason dug in his nails as the thought of Sheila and their son ran a marathon through his head.

"She died while giving birth to our baby. She lost a lot of blood. The baby died too. I lost two precious people in one day. It was hard to bounce back, because I didn't know what to do. I didn't have anyone to turn to. Me and Savion were beefing at the time, and I didn't know where he was. Like I told you before, me and Goon weren't tight anymore. Sheila and I had a house in Tracy and the owners helped me through my loss. The guy who introduced Sheila and me was there, but I needed family. So I sought after Savion, and when I found him, he was neck deep in shit, but he was all I had left."

"What happened to your parents?"

Jason leaned his head back and stared at the ceiling.

"My father was shot dead in front of me and my mother died of AIDS a few years ago," he whispered.

Christian held his hand tightly.

"I'm sorry," she said.

Jason sat his glass on the coffee table.

"Don't be. We all make our own choices. I'm not saying it doesn't hurt, but that's the choice they made. My mother was a smart woman and taught me a lot. She's the reason I'm intelligent. She pushed books on me. After I saw my pops get killed, I damn near became mute. I didn't talk that much, so Moms made me write my feelings out on paper. I stayed doing that and reading a lot of books at the same time."

"How did you survive?"

Jason stood up and walked to the window.

"I sold dope. Goon and I sold a lot of cocaine. You pretty much know the rest, but I miss my dude. I wish we could go back to the old days where we didn't care about the fame and all the spoils of the game. All me and Goon cared about was eating. That was it! I still do, Christian. It seems like every time I get out, it calls me right back, in some way, form, or fashion. But it is how I eat. It's what got me comfortably away from the headaches of a nine to five job. I thought I was out, but this is what I know until my writing career takes off. I'm not big on excuses, so you either take it or leave it. You wanted to know who you're dealing with, there it is."

Christian looked up at him as he stared at her.

Jason knelt down in front of her and took her hands in

his.

"Do you understand why I haven't told you anything? It's deep, very deep. I hurt, Christian, but I deal with it in my own way."

"You run," she said, looking into his eyes.

"You run from your problems. Not talking about things is a form of running, Jason. You can't cut the world off whenever you see fit. There are people you affect. People other than you that think about you and care for you. But on the flip-side, I understand. I understand you now."

"Do you?"

Christian nodded.

"A lot more than I did yesterday."

They both giggled at the remark.

"Jason, I'm with you. You want a lot of the same things that I want, and I'm in love with the fact that you're not afraid to do what you have to do while still being you at the same time. That is the one thing that Goon was missing. He became someone else in the process. What you do doesn't bother me because I see the way you do it. You're not consumed by it. The style most cats get down with, you know that ended up to be him. I got beat up when I questioned him and I'm not gonna count the times I caught him with other women in my own bed. You do it for the reasons it was meant to be done, surviving the only way you know how. I'm not mad at that. But you can't do it forever."

Jason nodded.

"I know. Really, I'm done with it, but I have one piece of that life left to deal with."

"What's that?"

"I have to go see somebody I trusted, then I can say I'm done."

Christian pursed her lips and kissed his cheek.

"Anything you need me for, I'm here. I can't be Sheila, but I can promise to have your back and hold you down when you need it, if you'll have me."

Jason stared at her lips as a million thoughts ran through

his mind. Trust seemed to glisten in her eyes as he ran his fingers through her hair.

"We'll see where it goes. That's all we can do, right?"

Christian smiled as she took his face in her hands.

"Come here, sexy. I have been missing this face for so long," she said as she kissed him softly.

"Thank you," Jason said, between kisses.

"For what?"

Jason stood up and took her in his arms.

"For listening. You don't know how important that is for someone to listen without judging you."

"Well, Mr. Wright, you walk out on me again, there isn't going to be any talking or listening. I'ma really get ghetto on you."

Jason started laughing.

"Girl, your square ass wouldn't know the least thing about getting gutter. By the way, it's gutter. Ghetto is too over-used."

"Oh," Christian said. "And I'm the square one? I got crazy love for you, Jason. I never thought I could miss somebody so bad. I feel what Beyoncé is talking about now, being dangerously in love. Not that I love you, but I understand what she was saying."

"You're gonna fight saying you love me with all your might, huh?"

Christian kissed his cheek, lips and forehead.

"A girl can't give up all of herself too soon."

Jason looked around the room and then back at her. He knelt down and picked her up by her thighs.

"I bet you give all of yourself tonight. I want to play a game with you."

Christian wrapped her arms around his neck.

"What would that be?"

Jason smirked as his hands held each one of her butt cheeks.

"Who will make the next one scream first?."

CHAPTER 31

Jill Scott's "Beautifully Human" CD played in the stereo as Italy bagged up ounces of weed. Tanya sat by, reading the latest copy of *King Magazine*.

"I know men don't actually believe all this stuff that the women are saying in the magazine," said Tanya. "Every girl doesn't like being approached like this or even touched like this."

Italy tuned her out as she weighed out the buds on her electrical scale. After the proper weight, she put the weed in zip lock bags, pressed out all the air, then wrapped them in cellophane.

"Damn, that is potent. What's that, a pound?" Tanya asked.

Italy didn't answer.

"Italy, do you hear me talking to you?"

Italy snapped out of her trance. "What did you say?"

Tanya put down her magazine and stood over her.

"What're you thinking about girl?"

"Nothing," Italy said, wrapping the last ounce.

Tanya smacked her lips.

"Girl please, you ain't never this quiet. What's up?"

Italy stuffed the packages in her Louis Vuitton Bag.

"I just have a lot on my mind."

"Since when you couldn't talk to me about what's on your mind? Speak about what's on your mind. Speak up now."

Italy zipped the bag and tossed it on the couch.

"My mother will be dead in I don't know how long. She's really sick. That disease is kicking in tough. I had to move her to the hospital a week ago. It's only been a few months since she told me she had the sauce. I went to see her in the hospital last night, and I didn't even recognize her. She was so thin. Some of her hair fell out too. I felt bad for all the bad things I said to her when we would fight. I wish we had more time to be a mother and daughter. Before she had to go in, it was beautiful. We really bonded. Now that *that* is over, it's like…*dag!* What am I gonna do? She told me to keep hustling and get in school. I went down to Chabot the other day, and Kamal's dog ass was there with all his friends. Girl, I just ran. It felt like high school all over again.

"They all started cat calling and pointing and shit. I didn't even want to get started on that tip again. So school is up in the air. Plus, I got bills to pay. I gotta keep this apartment unless I move to some place cheaper. I was thinking Sacramento or something like that. I miss my momma, Tanya, for real. It's like I need her more than ever right now."

Tanya sat down next to her.

"Well I really don't know what to say. But be happy that you two made up and got cool before she passed away. Imagine how that would have been had you not reached out to her."

"I know," Italy said, pouring a glass of water.

"Just let the good times you guys had live on in your heart. Good always outshines the bad. Stay by her side until that day comes. Remember, you're never alone. I know me and my family will have your back. Really, I don't want to see you selling weed, but I understand you have to get paid. My advice would be to get into some kind of school. You know what you want to take already, so go for it. I feel you on the Kamal issue, but fuck him. You can't even let that get to you, even though it will, because you're human, but clown his ass back. Tell him he has a little dick and can't fuck, in front of everybody. Fight fire with fire, you dig?"

"Thanks girl. I needed that."

Tanya hugged her and shook her shoulders.

"We gone make it, baby. We're queens."

Italy patted her hand.

"I saw Jason at the school."

"What?" Tanya said. "Did you talk to him?"

Italy shook her head slowly.

"No. He was with this girl. She was pretty too. They were all hugged up. I didn't even bother. I could've used his help dealing with Kamal's ass. I hope he's happy. He looked happy. I've seen the girl a few times. She's real pretty."

Tanya shook her head,

"Well, it isn't like you didn't have your chance. That's who you should've called before it all hit the fan. You'd probably be a lot happier."

"I know, but I couldn't. Jason has this way about himself. He can be so caring, but the way he cares makes me feel small. He isn't afraid to speak his mind and speaking his mind about the things I do isn't on my best liked list."

"You should've seen him at the hospital when Savion got killed. I have never seen someone look so hurt. The cops did him way bad. I heard them talking about Jason was under investigation about some drugs. They said they didn't have much on him though."

"Well, I hope he stays safe. That's all I can say. I'ma always remember him. He's a man in every sense of the word, from the good to the bad."

"You should call him, just to see how he's doing."

"Naw, life goes on. I met a Jason Wright once, I'll meet another one down the road."

"That's right," Tanya said, as the phone rang.

Tanya watched Italy's smiling face fade into a frown as she told someone she was on her way and quickly hung up the phone.

Italy rushed to get her bag and coat. “Get your coat, my mom is losing it. It’s kicking in real bad right now. Hurry up. I pray she’s not gone by the time we get there.”

CHAPTER 32

Beth's eyes were closed as she lay with an air mask over her face. Italy and Tanya each held one of her hands as she slept. Her stomach heaved up and down as if she was fighting for air.

"The doctor said she's hanging on by a string," Tanya said, looking down at her. "They're doing everything they can."

"I know," said Italy. "It just seems like it's never enough when death is the case. Are you going to be working tonight?"

Tanya nodded.

"Why? Do you want to go home and get some things?"

"Yeah, I gotta drop the stuff off too. I don't want to sit in here with it all in my bag. I know doctors have noses like Basset Hounds."

Beth's eyes blinked open. Italy noticed the yellowish color her brown eyes had become. Italy lightly ran her hand over her head.

"Hey Momma; how you feeling?"

Beth took the oxygen mask off her face.

"I need a drink," she said, groggily. "Can you get me a JD?"

Italy smiled. "Hell naw, Momma."

Tanya laughed.

"Alcohol and medicine don't mix."

Beth struggled to sit up, but finally gave up. Italy pressed a button to raise the top of the bed. Andy Griffith came on the TV making Beth grimace at the annoying whistle.

"Turn that damn TV off, please. I don't need to be reminded how old I am."

Tanya pressed the off button on the remote.

"Thank you. Girl, I hurt all over. How long y'all been standing here?"

"We have been here for about an hour," said Italy. I was gonna go home and get some things and stay the night with you."

Beth raised her hand slowly, and patted Italy's.

"You don't have to do that. I know how much you hate hospitals. Did you register in school yet?"

Tanya took that as her cue to leave. "I'll be back later. I'ma go check in and change clothes. No liquor, Momma B. I mean it!"

"Girl you are so mean," Beth said as Tanya walked out of the room. Silence took over the space as the door clicked shut.

"You didn't answer my question," said Beth, staring at Italy.

"I went down there," Italy said, sitting down. "I had a few problems."

"What kind of problems? They won't let you in?"

"Naw, that's not it. It was Kamal and his friends. It made the whole experience messed up. I was so happy and ready, then that."

Beth swallowed hard.

"I don't know what you seen in that boy. I knew he was bad news the moment you brought him home. Remember when I caught you two in your room?"

Italy laughed at the memory.

"It seems so long ago. Where has the time gone?"

"Hopefully to heaven. I know I haven't been too cool of a human being, but I hope God understands. Lord knows I apologize for my wrongs."

"It hasn't been all that bad. He has forgiven you. He might not be a '*he*.' He might be a '*she*,' and then you'll really be understood."

They both laughed a little.

"Italy baby," said Beth. "I want you to do something for me."

"What's that?" Italy asked, grabbing Beth's hands.

Tears began to flow out of Beth's smokey, yellowish eyes as she spoke.

"Survive. Survive well. Don't turn out like me. One of the reasons I got back in touch with you was because I saw you were going through the same stuff that I'd gone through. My momma didn't care about me for a while. She died with us not speaking. I didn't want us to end up like that. I want you to remember the times we had when I was clean. I know you won't forget the bad, but put the good over that."

"I will, Momma. I'm not ready for this. I'm not ready for you to die."

"Well baby, you don't really have a choice. God is ready for me. I'm not going to make it through the night. I feel it. When he calls, we don't have a choice but to go."

Italy nodded as she wiped the tears away.

"This has all happened for a reason. Look how close we've become over this time. I hate that it took this long for us to get right. We could've been well off by now."

"Italy, use this to strengthen you. Don't let it break you down. Number one, let it be an example that you must practice safe sex. Number two, let it be an example of what happens when you give up. I was thinking about your daddy earlier today. We used to be good together. I wish he wouldn't have been such an idiot, but I forgive him. I just wish he could see how beautiful you've turned out. Try and find him. I know it'll hurt, but find him. You need him. There's certain things a girl needs from a father. You need those things more than ever now. Please don't look for love in these silly little boys out here. Let it come to you. It will. Just be patient and take care of you.

"I don't want you out there settling for less because it's convenient. There are so many things I would change, but I can't. A parent's main responsibility is to make sure their child doesn't make the same mistakes they did. So let my last words be that of a parent to a child who will listen and understand."

Italy wiped her eyes and sat down in the chair next to the bed. Beth watched her every move.

"I need a cigarette, bad," Beth said, groggily.

"You know that ain't happening."

"I know. At least I tried."

"I feel weak, Momma."

"Do you think you're weak?"

"For certain things, yeah."

"Like what?"

"Love and a better life."

"Do you think you can get that for yourself?"

"I don't know. Not without help or going for what I know."

"You know a lot of things."

"I just don't want to be 35 or 40 years old, just getting it, though."

"Everything is a sacrifice, baby. Ball players have to sacrifice their youth. Rappers sacrificed their time. Actors… you get the point? Italy, go to fashion school. It's your niche."

"I'm trying to figure out what else to do besides go to school. What will come after?"

"Well, that can take some time, but you'll get it."

Beth felt her chest become weaker as she exhaled. Her breathing became heavier as the air got thick and began choking her. She kept it all in as she watched Italy talk. Tears began streaming from her eyes as she clutched her chest. Beth tried to tell Italy she loved her, but the words wouldn't come out as she fought for air.

The fight was over as she felt her heart stop and her last breath escaped her lips. Italy looked at her mother's face. Beth's eyes were fixed on hers.

"Momma? *Momma!*" Italy yelled.

Italy jumped to her feet and shook Beth slowly. Italy collapsed on her as she sobbed. She crawled onto the bed with her mother and wrapped her arm around her shoulder. Italy shut her mother's eyes and began rocking slowly from side to side. She looked towards the window as the last stretch of sunlight was squeezed away. In the silence, she prayed for her mother's spirit.

CHAPTER 33

Jason stood on top of a roof adjacent to the building he was watching. The September night breeze blew wild as he tightened the buttons on his leather coat as he waited for Bino's car to pull into the driveway of his mistress's apartment building. Jason knew Bino's schedule, and knew he was a man of predictability. The .380 he was carrying rested unnoticeably in his pocket. His mind drifted off to Savion as he watched his mistress light candles in the window.

He thought of the times his mother would hurry them off to church on Sundays and how they'd fight all day in the children's section. Jason smirked at the memory, knowing he missed Savion the most. Despite their differences, they always had each other's back, and Bino brought an end to that. The federal charges were dropped and he was left alone, so Bino told him.

Jason patiently waited out everything and threw on a dumb face and deaf ear to everything Bino said. He plotted out the day he'd avenge Savion with Bino's blood. For months, he waited and witnessed Bino give up a number of his associates in the process. The whole situation sickened him and he couldn't wait to put an end to him. As Bino's children got older, Jason fought the second-guessing within him. He felt for Trisha and the kids, but couldn't continue to fight the hate and disgust he had for Bino.

His phone vibrated in his pocket as he shook the thoughts from his head.

"What's up?" he said after reading Christian's number.

Christian's soft anxious voice calmed his nerves.

"Are you still coming by tonight?"

Jason smiled at the thought of the almost perfect time they'd been spending together. He willingly shared everything with her, and vice versa. Sheila seemed to sit on his shoulder whenever conflict showed itself. It seemed as if she had sent Christian herself.

"Yeah, I'm taking care of a few things right now, but I promise to be there by 11:00 tonight. Okay?"

"Well, hurry up, Mr. Wright. I bought something special I want you to see."

"Is it something to make me act a fool? Because if it ain't lace, I can't be at your place."

"Well you'll just have to come and see, right?"

Jason giggled as he thought about her body.

"I'll see you in a few hours, aiight?"

"Alright, Mr. Wright. Please bring a bag of chicken breasts and some fruit. I want to cook breakfast for you and don't want to interrupt anything with trips to the store."

"Okay! See you soon."

Jason turned off his phone and put it back in his pocket. He pulled his beanie back down over his ears and rubbed his gloved hands together while a strong gust of wind blew by him.

Jason took a step back as the lights from Bino's Jaguar LX appeared around the corner. He watched as he got out of the car and headed up the stairs with a bottle of champagne. Bino turned his head in every direction, checking for anything suspicious. Jason watched the streets for any sign of cars following him. His motorcycle was parked in front of the building next to the mistress' place. Bino paid it no attention as he headed into the building.

Jason flipped his collar up and headed down the stairs to the street. He walked briskly across to the building. He shut the foyer door slowly, not letting it click. The lights from the hallway were bright as he focused his eyes down the corridor. A light fixture hung from each end of the hallway. Jason unscrewed the glass covers slowly, and unscrewed the bulbs in each of the fixtures leaving the hallway pitch black. He put his ear to the door. Nothing could be heard but the Anthony Hamilton CD playing on the stereo. Jason took post in the shadows and waited for Bino to come out.

CHAPTER 34

An hour and a half passed, and Jason grew restless. Nobody seemed to be home, because no one entered or exited the building the whole time he waited. Jason walked back and forth to the door, listening to the sounds coming from behind. Moans and rocking furniture filled the space, while he contemplated knocking on the door and going in to kill both of them, but decided against it.

He looked at his watch: 9:30 p.m. He put his ear to the door one more time, then stepped outside into the shadows next to the building and lit a cigarette.

This is taking way too long, he thought.

He ducked into the shadows more as a car drove by, slowing in front of the building, then speeding off. Jason became nervous. The red alarm light flicked on and off on the dashboard of the Jaguar. Jason stepped close to the car.

A beep went off as he stood next to the window.

"Step away from the car," the alarm said, as he looked in the window. The car beeped three times as Jason stubbed his cigarette out and banged his fist on the driver's door. The alarm went off like a siren as he stepped back into the shadows.

After a minute, Bino came out in a pair of shorts with his keys. Jason saw the shine of the .45 in his hand as he looked up and down the street. Bino turned the alarm off while Jason gripped the handle of his survival knife. He held the knife close to this body as he crept slowly out of the shadows behind Bino who slowly climbed the stairs.

Bino tucked the gun in his waistband as Jason moved in, catching him off guard. Bino screamed as he tried to reach for the gun. Jason stabbed him in the hand, making Bino scream louder as Jason pulled the gun out of his waistband and threw it out the door. Jason kicked him back into the apartment as the mistress came from the bedroom.

Jason pulled out his .380 and shoved it in her face before she could say a word.

"Scream and it goes off. Sit down."

The curvy Mexican woman did as she was told.

Bino wiggled on the floor, trying to hold his hand together.

"Jason, what are you doing?" Bino asked, almost in a whisper.

Jason pulled him up and threw him on the couch next to the girl. Bino looked at Jason in shock.

"Have you lost your mind?"

Jason smacked Bino across the face with the butt of the gun.

"Shut up. You scream again and you die. You know what this is about. You ratted on Sav and got him killed."

Bino shook his head slowly as Jason held the gun to his side.

"Jason, I had to. They were going to put me away for life. They worked a deal if I gave them Savion. He was going to either get caught or die anyway, you know that. Be happy I kept your name out of it all."

Jason bit his lip and shook his head.

"You want to know the crazy part? What's crazy is I put my own family behind you. You always came first, Bee. You were like a father to me."

"And I still am, Jason. Put the gun down and let's work

this out. I'm not upset with you. I understand, but we can work this out."

Jason continued shaking his head. The girl started moving her hand under the couch cushion. Jason watched her out of the corner of his eye. He moved in lightning speed to the couch, grabbed a pillow, held the gun to it, and pulled the trigger. The pillow muffled the sound as the girl flopped back on the couch and slumped over. Feathers from the pillow blew in the air as blood poured slowly from the single shot to her left temple.

Bino jumped in his seat.

"Maria," he whispered stroking her hair slowly as he looked up at Jason. "Now we are beyond talking. You've fucked up now, boy. You better leave the state while you still can."

Jason tossed the pillow and picked up another.

"You're right. We're past talking."

Bino tried to scream his name out, but he was met by two bullets. Jason watched as he slumped to the floor with his eyes wide open, looking up at him. Jason threw the pillow on the floor and walked out of the apartment, shutting the door quietly.

The hallway was still dark and all the doors were closed. No one seemed to see or hear anything. Jason walked quickly to the rain gutter on the corner and tossed the gun down the drain. The knife rested in his pocket as he walked back to his motorcycle. He put his helmet on, started the bike, and sped away for the Bay Bridge.

Carlton Brown

CHAPTER 35

The lap top screen glowed brightly as Jason's fingers moved over the keys. He took a break and leaned back in his chair, glancing over the first chapters to his book, which seemed to flow from him in rapid speed. He glanced back in the darkness at Christian sleeping in his bed. He picked up a picture of the two of them framed next to the computer.

Ghosts of his family seemed to sit in the room as he took a deep breath. He began thinking of Sheila as he sat the picture back down. The first two chapters of his book detailed their love and growing oneness. By choosing to write about the women that have been in his life, and what their personalities did for him, it seemed as if the book wrote itself. Jason took another breath and spoke to all of them in whispers.

"Thank you, Momma. Thank you for force-feeding me this talent. Watch over Savion. Make sure he's not acting a fool up there and make sure Daddy keeps his foot on his neck. Help Sheila to raise my son to be an upstanding young man. I don't know when God plans to bring me home, but I hope to have a little more time here."

"What're you thinking about?" Christian asked, wrapping her arms around his shoulders.

"What're you doing up?"

"I had to use the bathroom. How's it coming?"

"Good, it's writing itself."

"When are you going to write about me?"

Jason laughed.

"Who said I was gonna write about you?"

"Oh please, Jay. I'm one of the best things to ever happen to you. You can't help but to."

Jason nodded.

"Later. I'm trying to get everyone else out of the way first. Did you finish your psych paper?"

"Yeah. You know that teacher really misses you. He's bored without your insight."

"He'll get over it. I just don't have the time for school right now. I talked to him two days ago. He still tries to pick my mind in every conversation."

"He started to pick on me because he knows we're together. Like you rubbed off on me or something."

"I hope I do."

"A little bit. You know you have that charm about yourself. It's too much for a girl to ignore."

Christian kissed his cheek and sat on Jason's lap.

"You gotta bend sometimes, Mr. Wright. Everything can't be about you."

Jason rubbed her thigh as he laughed.

"Feel free to leave anytime you're ready."

"Would you let me go?"

"You don't expect me to answer that, do you?"

"Yes I do."

"No way," Jason smirked. "If you don't kill anything, nothing dies," Jason said, rising from his chair.

Christian frowned and pulled her shorts over her stomach.

"Answer the question, Jason. If you can't, that means you're not sure of me or us."

Jason's smile faded. The silence between the two grew

thick.

"You're serious?"

"As a heart attack," Christian said, standing in front of him.

Jason smiled, shaking his head.

"I thought you were above asking questions you already know the answer to."

"I am."

"Then why this? Is there something else you're holding in?"

Christian bit her lip as she looked into his eyes.

"Where is this going, Jason? Really? Are we serious or are we just floating? Am I just convenient for you while you wander through life?"

"Where is this coming from?" Jason asked.

"It's coming from a woman you don't listen to. A woman who has to get on the train of Jason Wright or get passed up. Jason, you're everything I want in a man, but I can't keep switching myself to keep up with you. I'm starting to lose touch with me."

Jason met her eyes with ice.

"You seem to be the same person to me, except for right now. I haven't asked you to change anything or do anything to damage your integrity. Anything you're doing differently is your choice. Not my force."

His voice was calm.

Christian sat down in the chair and stared at him in silence.

"I asked you to stop selling drugs, you ignored me. I asked you to stay in school, you ignored me. The things that are most important, you ignore. Like what I say doesn't matter."

"So is this about having control over me?" Jason asked, his voice becoming enraged.

Christian matched his tone.

"No, it's not about control, Jason, it's about respect. Respect for your girl, *your woman*. Do you think I want to be one of those women going to see their man in the pen? Do you think I want to see you like your Uncle Champ?"

"Chris, I already explained my situation. I explained from the gate that this is what I do. You said you could handle it. Obviously, you spoke too soon. What's the point of me going school? I know what I want to do."

"Yeah, write a book you're too emotionally unstable to write. You think I don't hear you crying whenever you write about Sheila or your momma? You're too smart for this, Jason."

"Well it's all I have right now! You don't know half the shit I've been through. Instead of being selfish and thinking only about Christian, think about Jason and the things I've had to endure within the last few years. Matter of fact, you don't have to think about anything. I know how to be by myself. It seems it always ends up that way anyway."

"See there you go pushing me away again. Do you love me Jason?" Christian asked as tears began to stream from her eyes.

"I can't believe we're having this conversation," Jason said, turning his back.

Christian sprang from her chair and grabbed his arm.

"Answer the question, Jason. Do you love me?"

Jason turned to face her. His look became somber as they stared at each other in silence.

Christian wiped the tears from her eyes as she nodded her head.

"I thought so."

Jason looked away from her.

"I can't compete with a ghost, Jason. Just know that I did love you, and I will. Call me if you need me." Christian kissed his lips softly.

Jason stood still while she put on her coat, grabbed her keys, and let the apartment door slam behind her.

CHAPTER 36

Italy drove her new Toyota Avalon down East 14th in East Oakland. Sade's "Promise" CD played in the deck as her mind went in a million directions. She popped the top on a bottle of orange juice and took a long swallow. The urge to light a joint crossed her mind, but she fought it off, staying strong to her vow to quit.

As she approached 73rd, she looked at all the young black men on the corner, hustling. She recognized a few people and nodded in their direction as she approached a red light. A chubby dark skinned guy with a shiny bald head and a crisp goatee waved her down. She admired his clothes fitting well over his thick frame.

Italy let her passenger window down as he approached her car.

"What it do, Tone," she said, turning the music down.

"Shit! Nothing really. It's kind of slow. When you flip this?"

Italy ran her hand over the leather seats.

"Last week. My credit checked out and the money I stacked paid the down payment."

"That's right, girl. It's good to see you doing good. How's

Tanya?"

"Is that what you pulled me over for?"

"Keeping it real, hell yeah! You know I gotta keep tabs on her, even if we aren't together. She's too good for the bull-shit."

"Well, she's doing cool. Working hard. We just got a spot together in Union City. All she does is sleep and work."

"Is her new dude treating her cool?"

"That's none of your business, Tone," Italy laughed. "If you miss her that much, just call her. Her cell phone number is the same."

Tone nodded slowly.

Italy watched a pack of girls cross the street and walk to the corner. Italy noticed Bianca in a pair of daisy dukes, flirting with a few of the guys.

"Tone, is that girl new out here? The one in the shorts?"

Tone turned his head, smacking his lips.

"Hell naw. That's Bianca's hoe ass. Why, you know her?"

Italy thought back to their last conversation.

"Yeah, we used to kick it. Y'all running through her?"

"Like water. Everybody out here done touched that. What you doing kicking it with her?"

"Damn, you ask a lot of questions!"

Tone laughed as Bianca hugged him from behind. He shook her free and tapped the cars' doorframe.

"Tell Tanya I'ma call her, aiight. Be cool, Italy."

Bianca heard her name and bent down to meet her eyes.

"Italy? What's up, girl? Let me get in with you."

Italy put her car in drive.

"I don't have the time right now. I have something I'm already late for. Plus, I don't want to go backwards by beating your ass for that shit with Donovan. Be happy that I'm a different person now, Bee."

Bianca smacked her lips, catching Italy's vibe.

"I'll holla then," she said, walking back to the block.

Italy laughed as she turned the music back up and continued up the street. She exhaled as she came to 96th.

"Damn, you're lucky we got on good terms, Momma," she whispered to herself as she turned down the street until she came to D Street. She drove slowly, watching a few fiends walk quickly down the street as a few hustlers stood on the block, eyeing her car. She drove up to them and lowered her window.

"What's up y'all? Do y'all know a dude named Woody?"

"OG Woody?" one of them asked, revealing a row of gold teeth.

"Yeah, I guess," she said, putting the car in park.

"Yeah, he lives right behind you."

"Is he in the pen though?" one of the other guys asked the group.

They remained silent, shaking their heads.

"He should be there, beautiful," the man with the gold teeth said.

Italy put the car in reverse and parked in front of the house. The gate was leaning to the side on top of the dirt lawn. She slowly walked up the short steps and knocked on the door.

"Who is it?" She heard a deep voice ask.

"Italy," she said, barely audible.

Her throat became dry; she felt the nervousness creep into her stomach as the door slowly opened. Italy found herself staring up at a giant.

"May I help you?" he asked, staring down at her.

Italy fumbled with her words as she asked him,

"Are you Woody Stevens?"

"Yeah, what you need? I'm out of E-pills."

Italy's knees became weak as she realized she was face-to-face with her father. She searched his face for some familiar features.

"I'm Italy. I'm… I'm your daughter."

Woody leaned against the doorframe slowly.

"I was wondering when I'd see you. I heard Beth passed on."

Italy swallowed hard, noticing that she had the same facial expression as him when she became upset.

"You know she died and you still couldn't check on me?" Italy asked, visibly shaken.

Woody exhaled loudly as two fiends walked up the short steps.

"I ain't open yet. Come back in an hour," he yelled at them.

Italy watched them run back the way they came.

"Now, to answer your question, no. No I didn't."

Woody stood his caramel, 260 pound, 6'4" frame up, stepped outside and shut his door.

Italy became more upset at the fact that he didn't ask her to come in. She folded her arms over her chest as he sat on the arm of a chair sitting on the porch.

"Why not," she asked, breaking the silence.

"Because you're not my child," he said, lighting a cigarette.

Italy's heart dropped.

Woody inhaled deeply and blew the smoke into the air, looking up at her. Italy stared at his grey waves and thick grey beard.

"I'm sure Beth has told you a million times, her side of the story. But you look like you're smart enough to know there are two sides to everything."

Italy sat on the short steps. The urge to roll a joint and smoke it was stronger than ever. Woody continued smoking his cigarette.

"I'm listening," Italy said, becoming irritated. She braced herself for a verbal lashing from her mother.

"You're pretty," Woody said, flicking an ash from the cigarette. "You look like a lighter version of your Momma when she was young. Anyway, you are my biological baby. I see it now. You're like your grandma. She has that real fair skin like yours. At first, I couldn't see that. I've dealt with that for years until I finally buried it. Then I get word that Beth died of AIDS. My heart dropped a bit. Me and Beth had our problems, but I never stopped loving her.

"But life has its turns and both of our turns weren't good. I was smoking probably more than her. By the time I bounced back, you were already grown and I was in and out of jail. So instead of causing all kinds of madness, I just continued to go ahead with my life, knowing that blood will eventually find blood."

Italy felt the tears form in her eyes. She wiped them before they could drop.

"That isn't even a valid excuse."

"Well, what do you want me to say, Italy? Do you see how crazy this is right now? I have never been this damn nervous in my life. You think you feel weird. Have a child that you've only seen a few times, then tell me how you feel when you meet her in one piece and beautiful."

Italy smiled at the remark.

"You don't know half the things I've been through. Most times, I just needed a male figure to love me."

Woody lit another cigarette.

"If you're here to lay a guilt trip, you can save it."

Italy stood up and paced back and forth in front of him

"Are you serious? You desert your damn family and tell me to save my speech? You should already feel guilty. You're lucky I'm taking it this easy. I could blow up on you. I was woman enough to come see you. My momma asked me to find you and make amends."

"Well, I'm sorry to tell you, nothing's gonna change. My life isn't even together enough to try and make up for lost time. I'm your daddy, but I'm not your *father,* and I'm not trying to be, 23 years later. You'll only end up hurt more, because I'm not changing."

Italy looked down the block, thinking about her mother.

"You don't bite your tongue, huh? What did my mother see in you?"

Woody laughed as he exhaled the smoke. His eyes grew distant as he reminisced, thinking about the good times he had with Beth.

"Life is hard, Italy. You should never bite your tongue for anything. My belief is either you accept it or not. It wasn't always war between me and your momma. We were in love like crazy. But things change and people grow apart. I'm not one to badmouth the dead. God bless her soul, but it takes two people to split a relationship up. That's as far as I'll get into it. Like I said, I don't badmouth the dead."

They sat in silence for what seemed like an eternity.

"We have the same facial expressions," Italy finally said, smiling.

She cupped his face in her hands and kissed him on the forehead.

"I gotta go take care of some business. I'll be back through here in a couple of days."

Woody felt his body melt as her lips touched his head.

"What you coming back here for?" he asked surprised.

Italy tightened her jacket around her waist.

"Because no matter how much you try and push me away, I'ma force my way in your life. I need you just like you need me. You need someone to love and I need my daddy. I don't want anything from you. I have my own money. I'ma hustla! I guess it's in the blood. All I need is your love and guidance. You talk proper, so I know you're educated, and there are still things that I'm trying to understand. So, how you like that, pops?"

Woody was shocked. He laughed as he stood up.

"You're just like your mother, *bold*, very bold. That's one reason I loved her."

Woody looked at her quizzically. "You got any babies?"

Italy shook her head.

"Nope! No kids, no man. Not looking for either one, right now. I have way too much other stuff going on."

"What you selling?"

"We'll talk about it later. It's nothing big. Just weed."

Woody nodded his head.

"Can I hug you?" he asked, with his arms stretched out.

Italy smirked,

"Oh, you're all love now, huh?" she said, walking into his arms.

"We gone work it out, old man," she whispered as they embraced.

Woody felt his body shake as he held Italy tightly in his arms. Tears dropped from both of their eyes. In unison, they wiped them away as they released.

"I'll talk to you in a couple days," she said, walking out of the yard."

"Okay, I'll be waiting." Woody answered, shaking from the lovely reaction.

Italy started her car and rolled her window down.

"Daddy? Stop smoking. It really stinks."

Woody flipped her off as she drove away. Both smiled to themselves at how much they were alike.

CHAPTER 37

Jason pulled to up Tyrell Avenue and glanced down the block. Everything seemed dead, as only a few hustlers gripped the corner, trying to get off whatever they could. Champ looked around, trying to put together the action and thinking to himself that this would be a bogus run. Malikie sat on the porch to Beth's old apartment, text messaging a girl he was trying to get with. Jason cruised by slowly until he saw him, then parked the car. Malikie peeked up from his iPhone and watched Jason get out of the car.

Malikie couldn't contain the smile he flashed immediately after seeing Jason.

"What's good, bruh? I thought you were coming by when that business was handled? I been losing money like crazy, buying that bullshit these niggas been out here serving. I hope you have something good to tell me or else I'ma have to call my man over here to handle you."

Jason loved the fact that Malikie held a smile the whole time he talked, meaning every word he said.

"No need for any of that, Mal. I had a few things to deal with that were more important than getting that to you. But, my word is all I have, so here I am."

Malikie patted him on the shoulder as he continued to smile.

"So what you got for me?"

"I got a real good friend of mine who is OG, and all about business. I'ma put you on, but if anything goes foul, I will kill you myself. Do you hear me?"

Malikie's smile faded for the first time. He never liked to have his life threatened, but still, he understood the game and everything Jason was saying.

"You know what, bruh? I don't let anybody talk to me like that, but I dig your style, Jay. Plus, the fact that you showed up after all this time with a hook up, still says a lot. Trust that I mean business, and I never bite the good hand, bruh. The bad hand will get shot all day, you dig?"

Jason laughed and nodded.

"Well, come get in the car with me. My man is in the front seat. You two can handle everything. I will stand outside of the car."

The smile returned to Malikie's face as he patted Jason on the shoulder again.

"I like your style, Jay. I really do."

Months later, Jason's head pounded as he drove through the gates of Rolling Hills Cemetery. He parked his car, took off his shades and began to slowly massage his temples, staring in the mirror at the black circles around his eyes.

"Damn, I need to sleep," he whispered to himself.

He put his shades back on and stepped out of the car. He adjusted his black turtleneck sweater and zipped up the black leather coat as the wind started to blow.

The 36 roses he brought with him were scattered over the back seat. He bundled all of them up together and proceeded to the graves. A hint of sun came out as he got closer to the graves of Rochelle, Savion and Sheila. Jason adjusted his shades and slowed down as he looked around the cemetery. Leaves blew over his feet as the wind carried them over the graves of the dead.

"Damn, this feels like a movie, y'all," he giggled to himself. "What's up?" he said as he stood in front of the graves.

Jason placed twelve roses on each on their headstones and cleaned off the old roses.

"How y'all been doing up there? I know it's been a minute, I been kind of busy, working some things out with myself. Christian was right about one thing, as y'all know. I am too damn emotional. So I've been working on letting some of that go. I cried myself out writing that book, but it's finally finished. I got a book deal with it too. Yeah, they gave me some good money for three books. That's cool. Hopefully, they sell a little something so I can eat off this for good.

"I quit grinding. I was tired, Sav. That shit is too stressful. I got a regular 9 to 5. Can you believe I'm a damn welder? So I really need this book thing to crack, so I can quit that. I don't like all that damn fire. I moved into a nice apartment. The Feds questioned me about Bino's death. I couldn't care less. Let him rot in hell. I still look out for Trisha and the kids. It's not their fault their husband and daddy was a snake. It hurt for a minute, but I had to shake that. One thing I can't let ride is betrayal. It doesn't sit well with me and I couldn't even look at myself for a long time on that. Was I wrong, Momma? Is it wrong to be able to kill someone that easy?"

Jason looked up over the hills of graves. He saw a woman standing in front of a grave at the far end of the cemetery.

"Champ got me going to the mosque," Jason continued.

"Yeah, I've been studying Islam. It's kind of natural, right? As much as I talk of the good life and things concerning black people. It's good though. After this book deal gets situated, I was thinking about leaving the country for a couple of years. Maybe move to London or France. Allah said my earth is spacious, so go see it. I'd be able to see a lot over there, plus make my pilgrimage to Mecca.

"I want to set foot on African land. My man said there's nothing like it. It's like being connected. You just feel like you belong. I'm still sitting nice from the game, and I still drive that same old car and have the same old clothes. I'll treat myself to some new ones before I leave. I'm going to take a trip to London in a few weeks, so I wanted to put some fresh flowers down and talk a bit."

Jason bit his lip as he felt the tears fall down his cheeks.

"I miss y'all so much. I feel all alone out here. It's like I try to keep going and stay strong, but it's hard. I'm scared to love anything but myself. Sheila, is that crazy, baby? Me, scared to love? I miss you so much, Sheila. Yeah, I lost Christian, and she was good for me. I couldn't tell her I love her, so I guess I really didn't. I think she was a love substitute for you. It felt like she was asking too much of me. Like she was saying move on and forget about y'all. We all know I can't do that, y'all are my family.

"She called a few times, but I didn't return any of her calls. Hopefully, she likes the things I wrote about her in my book. A relationship isn't something I need right now. I need to be free to grow and live. I think that's what you were trying to tell me, Sav. I got it now, brotha. I got it now."

CHAPTER 38

"Woody is crazy, Momma. I'm glad you made me promise to find him. We've been kicking it pretty tough. I can't believe he's still in the game. I made him get a job, to get parole off his back, and I got him to quit smoking. All he needed was some love in his life. He's been miserable for so long, but he's coming around.

"I finally got into school. It's hella fun, too. I'm acing this course and my designs are coming out crazy. The teacher really likes my drive. Kamal and his boys still do the same little boy shit, but I just brush it off and keep going. It's died down now. I guess they see it doesn't bother me. I got a job at Macy's in Bayfair. I like it and you know I got a closet full of stuff. Me and Tanya's vibe is really good. We give each other space, so we get along. Plus, we're both neat freaks. She thinks she's in love again, but we'll see. I'm not getting into anything right now.

"I've never been this focused before in my life, and I like it. A lot of people I used to run with are doing bad, real bad. I'm glad I kept it moving and I'm glad we rekindled our relationship. I try to imagine what it would be like if you were still here, but then it starts to hurt, and I'm so tired of crying."

Italy wrapped her arms around her chest and looked

around. She noticed a man bending down at a gravesite near the top of the cemetery. She turned back around and stared long and hard at Beth's grave.

"I'm glad I don't feel alone anymore, Momma. I'm so happy I have my daddy here. He's so handsome too. Y'all would've looked good together. He's gonna move closer to me in Fremont. It's a brand new start for the both of us.

"I'm still selling weed, and yes I know, but Macy's doesn't pay enough to cover my bills. So I gotta do what I gotta do. Momma, it's been so cold out here, being a woman. I can see why you started doing what you were doing. It's like you had to numb the pain somehow. I'm still not smoking weed. My experiences have built up my character, so I don't need it. Shit, I don't even drink either. No vices. That's what Woody says makes you stronger. Carry no crutches and you have to face everything head on. I feel stronger already. Common courtesy gets you a long way.

"I've been hitting the gym real hard too. I just feel good, Momma. I thank you for the good and the bad. It made me who I am. Well, I'm about to get out of here. It's getting cold and I have to take Woody shopping. I love you Momma, but you already know that."

Italy arranged the flowers on the grave once more before walking off. She wiped the tears from her eyes as she walked with her arms folded over her chest.

At the same time, the man she had spotted earlier, walked away from the graves he was visiting with his head down from the gravestone. He stopped, raised his head, and whispered something before continuing with his head up. Italy stared at his face.

"I know him," she whispered, as she walked closer to him.

Italy smiled when Jason looked up at her. He stopped in his tracks, smiled and waved at her as she approached.

"Well, well, well," she said, giving him a hug. "If it isn't Mr. Wright."

Jason continued smiling as he kissed her cheek.

"How are you doing, Italy?" he asked, holding her shoulders.

"I'm fine, just visiting my mother. How about you?"

"My moms, Sheila, my son, and my brother are all buried here."

"Damn," Italy said, unconsciously.

Jason giggled.

Italy caught herself.

"I'm sorry. I didn't mean it like that."

Jason held his hands up.

"It's okay, it is kind of unbelievable."

They walked to their cars in silence. Jason sat on his hood as she stood in front of him.

"Damn, you still have the Mitt, huh? I think about you every time I see one of these on the street."

Jason tapped the hood for her to sit down next to him.

"Yeah, I can't get rid of it. I'm going to sell it soon, though. You know, I used to wonder what happened to you. What are you into now?"

"Work and school, that's it. I don't have the time for anything else. What about you?"

"Basically, the same thing over here. I just got a book deal, so I'm going to be pretty busy getting them done.

"What did you write about?"

"All the women that have been in my life. It came out good."

"How is your girlfriend?"

"Stop fishing, Italy."

Italy smiled.

"I'm not fishing. I seen you with this girl that goes to my school. Y'all looked really happy."

"You go to Chabot?"

Italy nodded.

Jason sighed,

"Well things didn't work out. I have no hard feelings, because she's really a good girl and a very, very good person."

"You seem more happy now, Jason. I see a lot more smiling and openness."

Jason nodded.

"You too. I haven't heard anything about a silly nigga."

"Oh no! There won't be any of that. The only man in my life is my daddy. He's enough to deal with. But that smile looks real good on you. You need to keep it up. All that frowning you used to do made you look scary as hell."

Jason laughed. They sat in silence, looking over all the graves.

"It's crazy, huh?" Jason said, looking at her.

"What's that?"

Jason stood up and stretched.

"That death is the one thing that's certain in our lives. What did your mom die of?"

Italy looked away to the graves. "AIDS," she said in a whisper.

Jason stopped in his tracks.

"Did you say AIDS?"

Italy nodded.

"Mine too. My mom died of AIDS too."

"I guess we do have something in common, after all."

Jason nodded as he looked at all the graves. They sat in silence again, staring at what seemed to be nothing.

"Do you want to go get something to eat? I'm hungry." Jason said, cutting his eyes at her.

Italy stood up and hugged him again.

"Give me your number and I'll call you tonight. We can eat then. Right now, I gotta meet my daddy."

Jason put his number in her phone as they walked to her car. Italy couldn't keep her eyes off him.

"What?" Jason said, feeling her stare.

"I'm over here wondering what this dinner is going to turn into. You know there is a reason we keep bumping into each other."

Jason smiled as he looked back over the graves. Italy's flirting brought a much needed smile to his day.

"Yeah, they say everything happens for a reason. We'll just have to see, right?"

Italy bit her bottom lip, trying to hide the feeling coming over her.

"Yeah, we'll see, Jason. Call me later if I don't call you first."

Jason stood at his car as he watched Italy drive off. He waved at her as the car disappeared over the hills.

CHECK OUT THESE LCB SEQUELS

LCB BOOK TITLES

See More Titles At
www.lifechangingbooks.net

BEST-SELLING AUTHOR
KENDALL BANKS
DOES IT AGAIN WITH FILTHY
RICH PART 1 AND 2!
PART 3 IS ON THE WAY!

In Stores Now

ORDER YOUR COPY TODAY!!!

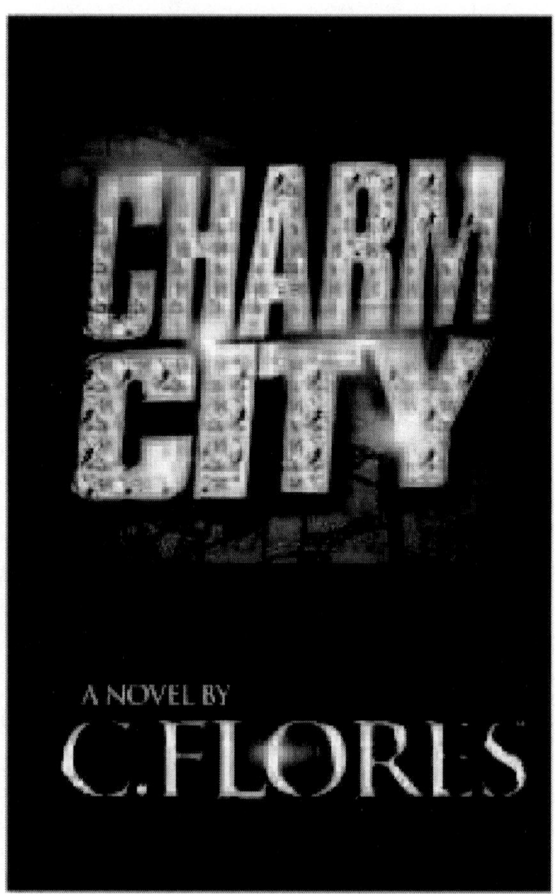

Danette Majette Presents

I Shoulda Seen Him Comin'

Part 1 and 2!

ORDER FORM

MAIL TO:
PO Box 423
Brandywine, MD 20613
301-362-6508

Ship to:	
Address:	
City & State:	Zip:

Date:	Phone:
Email:	

Make all money orders and cashiers checks payable to: Life Changing Books

Qty.	ISBN	Title	Release Date	Price
	0-9741394-2-4	Bruised by Azarel	Jul-05	$ 15.00
	0-9741394-7-5	Bruised 2: The Ultimate Revenge by Azarel	Oct-06	$ 15.00
	0-9741394-3-2	Secrets of a Housewife by J. Tremble	Feb-06	$ 15.00
	0-9741394-6-7	The Millionaire Mistress by Tiphani	Nov-06	$ 15.00
	1-934230-99-5	More Secrets More Lies by J. Tremble	Feb-07	$ 15.00
	1-934230-95-2	A Private Affair by Mike Warren	May-07	$ 15.00
	1-934230-96-0	Flexin & Sexin Volume 1	Jun-07	$ 15.00
	1-934230-89-8	Still a Mistress by Tiphani	Nov-07	$ 15.00
	1-934230-91-X	Daddy's House by Azarel	Nov-07	$ 15.00
	1-934230-88-X	Naughty Little Angel by J. Tremble	Feb-08	$ 15.00
	1-934230820	Rich Girls by Kendall Banks	Oct-08	$ 15.00
	1-934230839	Expensive Taste by Tiphani	Nov-08	$ 15.00
	1-934230782	Brooklyn Brothel by C. Stecko	Jan-09	$ 15.00
	1-934230669	Good Girl Gone bad by Danette Majette	Mar-09	$ 15.00
	1-934230707	Sweet Swagger by Mike Warren	Jun-09	$ 15.00
	1-934230677	Carbon Copy by Azarel	Jul-09	$ 15.00
	1-934230723	Millionaire Mistress 3 by Tiphani	Nov-09	$ 15.00
	1-934230715	A Woman Scorned by Ericka Williams	Nov-09	$ 15.00
	1-934230685	My Man Her Son by J. Tremble	Feb-10	$ 15.00
	1-924230731	Love Heist by Jackie D.	Mar-10	$ 15.00
	1-934230812	Flexin & Sexin Volume 2	Apr-10	$ 15.00
	1-934230748	The Dirty Divorce by Miss KP	May-10	$ 15.00
	1-934230758	Chedda Boyz by CJ Hudson	Jul-10	$ 15.00
	1-934230766	Snitch by VegasClarke	Oct-10	$ 15.00
	1-934230693	Money Maker by Tonya Ridley	Oct-10	$ 15.00
	1-934230774	The Dirty Divorce Part 2 by Miss KP	Nov-10	$ 15.00
	1-934230170	The Available Wife by Carla Pennington	Jan-11	$ 15.00
	1-934230774	One Night Stand by Kendall Banks	Feb-11	$ 15.00
	1-934230278	Bitter by Danette Majette	Feb-11	$ 15.00
	1-934230299	Married to a Balla by Jackie D.	May-11	$ 15.00
	1-934230308	The Dirty Divorce Part 3 by Miss KP	Jun-11	$ 15.00
	1-934230316	Next Door Nympho By CJ Hudson	Jun-11	$ 15.00
	1-934230286	Bedroom Gangsta by J. Tremble	Sep-11	$ 15.00
	1-934230340	Another One Night Stand by Kendall Banks	Oct-11	$ 15.00
	1-934230359	The Available Wife Part 2 by Carla Pennington	Nov-11	$ 15.00
	1-934230332	Wealthy & Wicked by Chris Renee	Jan-12	$ 15.00
	1-934230375	Life After a Balla by Jackie D.	Mar-12	$ 15.00
	1-934230251	V.I.P. by Azarel	Apr-12	$ 15.00
	1-934230383	Welfare Grind by Kendall Banks	May-12	$ 15.00
	1-934230413	Still Grindin' by Kendall Banks	Sep-12	$ 15.00
	1-934230391	Paparazzi by Miss KP	Oct-13	$ 15.00
	1-93423043X	Cashin' Out by Jai Nicole	Nov-12	$ 15.00
	1-934230634	Welfare Grind Part 3 by Kendall Banks	Mar-13	$15.00
	1-934230642	Game Over by Winter Ramos	Apr-13	$15.99
	1-934230618	My Counterfeit Husband by Carla Pennington	Aug-14	$ 15.00
	1-93423060X	Mistress Loose by Kendall Banks	Oct-13	$ 15.00
	1-934230626	Dirty Divorce Part 4	Jan-14	$ 15.00
	1-934230596	Left for Dead by Ebony Canion	Feb-14	$ 15.00
	1-934230456	Charm City by C. Flores	Mar-14	$ 15.00
	1-934230499	Pillow Princess by Avery Goode	Aug-14	$ 15.00
			Total for Books	$
			Shipping Charges (add $4.95 for 1-4 books*)	$
			Total Enclosed (add lines)	$

* Prison Orders- Please allow up to three (3) weeks for delivery.

Please Note: We are not held responsible for returned prison orders. Make sure the facility will receive books before ordering.

*Shipping and Handling of 5-10 books is $6.95, please contact us if your order is more than 10 books. (301)362-6508